APRIL AND THE DRAGON LADY

HARCOURT BRACE & COMPANY · 1919–1994 · SEVENTY-FIVE YEARS

LENSEY NAMIOKA

April

AND THE

DRAGON
LADY

Browndeer Press

Harcourt Brace & Company

San Diego   New York   London

Requests for permission to make copies of any part of
the work should be mailed to: Permissions Department,
Harcourt Brace & Company, 6277 Sea Harbor Drive,
Orlando, Florida 32887–6777.

Library of Congress Cataloging-in-Publication Data
Namioka, Lensey.
April and the Dragon Lady/Lensey Namioka.
p.   cm.
"Browndeer Press."
Summary: Feeling confined by the traditional family
attitudes of her strong-willed, manipulative grandmother,
sixteen-year-old April Chen fights for her independence.
ISBN 0-15-276644-8
ISBN 0-15-200886-1 (pbk.)
[1. Chinese Americans — Fiction. 2. Grandmothers — Fiction.]
I. Title.
PZ7.N1426Ap   1994
[Fic] — dc20   93-27958

Designed by Camilla Filancia
First edition   A B C D E

Printed in Hong Kong

To the memory of my mother,

who was all yang

—L. N.

APRIL AND THE DRAGON LADY

ONE

*H*E WAS A tall redhead, skinny, with big hands and feet. I thought he looked familiar. His smile cracked his face wide open. "Hi. You're April Chen, right? We bumped into each other. Literally."

Then I remembered. I had gone on my first Rock Hounds outing three weeks ago, and we had been hunting around the base of Mount Pilchuck. With a spurt of excitement, I had spotted something on the ground. It looked like a big, lumpy potato, but from the texture of the surface I was pretty sure it was a geode, a rock with a hollow inside which might contain beautiful crystals. I had rushed over and bent down to snatch it.

Someone else had spotted the geode at exactly the same time, and our heads had met with a crack. Even now, just thinking about it made my ears ring.

"Oh, yeah," I said. "You're . . . uh . . . Steve Daniels, right?"

"Right!" He took a rock from his backpack. It was the one we had both reached for. "I feel kind of mean, taking this while you were sitting on the ground, dizzy and everything."

"You have as much right to it as I have," I protested.

Steve held out the lump of rock. "A lump for a lump. And the lump on your head was bigger than mine. So you deserve it more."

His hands were large, but his fingers were deft as they moved lovingly over the rock. I didn't feel right about accepting his offer. On the other hand, he might be hurt if I refused it.

Then I had an idea. "Let's cut it open. Geodes are best when they're cut, anyway, so we can see what's inside. Then we can each take half."

Steve grinned again, and the freckles danced over his cheeks. "I was hoping you'd say that."

We were at a meeting of the Rock Hounds, held at the home of our science teacher, Mr. Cappelli, who had organized the club. I was a junior at Garfield High School, and of all my extracurricular activities, this was my favorite.

For years I had been fascinated by stones and rocks, which came in so many colors and patterns. At first I had been attracted to the ones with bright colors, such as jade and opal. After a while I became interested in the shapes of crystals, and the swirling patterns found in marble and gneiss. I particularly loved geodes, because they looked so drab and uninteresting on the outside, while often hiding bright, jewel-like stones inside.

Another reason I liked the Rock Hounds was because I felt comfortable with the other kids in the group. We shared a common interest, and we weren't trying to put each other down. I didn't enjoy school athletics, because it's always been difficult for me to be openly competitive.

Of course there was a certain amount of competition in the Rock Hounds, too. We were all eager to show Mr. Cappelli our finds. That was how Steve and I had met head on, after all. But it was a good-natured competition — splitting the geode was typical of the Rock Hounds.

Steve and I helped ourselves to more cookies and punch, and compared notes on interesting rocks we had met. I noticed immediately that I felt very relaxed with Steve. He poured himself on the sofa and sat there without a ripple. When he got up to get more cookies, I liked the way he moved without visible effort.

Considering the bumpy start of our relationship, things were improving fast. At ten o'clock, unfortunately, I felt that I had to go home.

"But it's still early!" Steve said. "Don't you want to stay while we decide where the Rock Hounds should go next week?"

He seemed really sorry to see me leave, and it gave me a nice warm feeling inside. "My grandmother is home alone," I told him. "I promised I wouldn't leave her too long."

Steve walked me to the door. "Have you got a car? Or is someone picking you up?"

I shook my head. "My dad is out of town, and my brother is studying late at the university. Don't worry, I can take the bus."

"I've got a car," Steve said quickly. "I can take you home. You shouldn't walk to the bus stop alone at this time of the night."

I accepted his offer in the end. To tell the truth, I was glad of the ride. It was raining hard, and like a true Seattle native I didn't carry an umbrella. It would be miserable squishing off to the bus stop, which was several blocks away.

We make a lot of jokes about the rain here. You can buy sweatshirts printed with "Seattle Rain Festival: Jan. 1 to Dec. 31," and there are bumper stickers that say, "We don't tan in Seattle. We rust." On the whole, our rain is steady but gentle. Tonight, though, it was pouring.

Steve had borrowed his brother's beat-up jalopy, and its sluggish windshield wipers couldn't keep up with the downpour. The car crept along slowly while Steve peered through the rain-streaked windshield.

"Your brother's at the university library tonight?" he asked. "Couldn't he study at home and watch over your grandmother?"

"He has an important problem set due tomorrow," I replied. "It's easier for him to concentrate at the library."

Steve glanced at me for a moment. "Is your grandmother an invalid?"

"Oh, no. There's nothing wrong with her. But lately she's started to wander around at night. We have to make sure she doesn't go too far."

It wasn't something I wanted to talk about, so I changed the subject. "I know a good place where I can get that geode cut and polished. You'll get your half, I promise."

We chatted comfortably. Then, when we came to our street, I suddenly felt a little shy. It was almost like being taken home after a date.

Up to now I had gone out only with Chinese-American boys. Should I invite Steve into the house? If I did, Grandma might see him. She wouldn't be pleased.

When the car pulled up in front of our house, I hesitated. Then I decided not to invite him in after all. "Thanks a lot for taking me, Steve," I said, getting out. "I'm sorry I made you leave early, too."

"I couldn't let my half of the geode escape into the night. Maybe we'll see each other in school tomorrow, okay?"

"Maybe we will," I replied. Watching his car sputter noisily down the block, I realized that I was smiling.

I had started to fish in my purse for the key to the front door when I heard the sound of a garbage can lid being replaced. The cans had been left in front of each house for collection the next morning, and the sound I had heard seemed to come from next door.

Then I heard quick, light steps. I tensed. A burglar, scouting the neighborhood? Why should he be looking into garbage cans?

A slight figure appeared, illuminated briefly

by the streetlight, and darted away from the garbage can next door. I blinked my eyes in the rain. It couldn't be! But it was! It was my grandmother!

Carrying a big sack, Grandma walked to the garbage can of the next house down the street. She lifted the lid, took something out of the sack, and threw it inside.

What was she thinking of? By the time I started after her, she was already headed for the third house down.

"Grandma?" I cried, as I reached her. "What on earth are you doing?"

Grandma turned and shook her head. "Hush, don't yell. We don't want to wake the neighbors."

"But what — what have you got in that sack there? What are you throwing away?"

Grandma showed me the sack. It contained empty soap boxes, the ones that had stood in tottering piles against the wall of our dining room for almost a year.

"Harry said I was coughing because of the soap powder from these boxes," said Grandma. She threw one of the boxes into the can and put the lid quietly back. "He said I should get rid of them."

I suppose from Grandma's point of view, it

made perfectly good sense. Since our garbage can couldn't hold all the soap boxes, she naturally started filling the cans of our neighbors. She wasn't hurting anybody.

I tried to smile at her. "That's enough for tonight, Grandma. It's raining hard and you're wet. You'll catch cold." Gently taking the sack, I started walking up the block to our house.

Grandma sneezed. She didn't argue with me, but followed me home and entered the house. She was thoroughly soaked, and so was I. I hoped that her sneeze was from the soap powder, and not from a cold.

After Grandma had gone to her room, I looked around. Most of the boxes in the dining room were gone, and I could see a big empty space along the wall. That meant she must have spent a good part of the night going up and down the street, throwing boxes away into the neighborhood garbage cans.

In the middle of the room we used to have a dining set imported from Hong Kong, consisting of a table and eight chairs, all made of dark rosewood. Mother had been proud of the formal set, and it had been kept beautifully polished while she was alive. When Grandma's pile of soap boxes had started to grow, the table had been pushed to one side. We ate dinner sitting along three sides of the table, with Father and Grandma facing each other, while Harry and I faced the blank wall.

The pile got so high that I stopped bringing my friend Judy home. I didn't want her to think I had a loony grandmother. One day, after a spell of sneezing from the soap powder, I approached Father. "I'm proud of Grandma for saving all these paper bags, bottles, cartons, and stuff," I said, trying to be diplomatic. "But why doesn't she hand them over to the recycling truck?"

Father looked embarrassed. "This saving habit started in Chongqing during the Second World War, when we had to treasure every scrap of paper and metal. Apparently Grandma has gone back to the habits of her earlier years. Old people sometimes do this, you know."

When the piles of boxes had become waist high, both Father and I had suggested getting rid of them. But Grandma had refused. Now, one word from Harry, and out she went on a stormy night to throw the boxes away.

My brother, Harry, was the one she listened to because he was a grandson. I didn't count with her because I was only a granddaughter, a girl. Harry was the one who was expected to marry and produce sons to preserve the Chen name. There was nothing I could do about Grandma's attitude toward me, so I tried not to mind.

Grandma is getting more and more eccentric, I thought, as I brushed my teeth and prepared for bed. Saving soap boxes isn't so bad, but it's worse to go out in the middle of the night to throw them in other people's cans. On the other hand, it wasn't my place to criticize her for getting a little eccentric. The world would be a pretty boring place if we were all perfectly normal.

As I went back to my room, I heard the front door open. "Harry?" I called out. "Is that you?"

"It's not the Easter Bunny," said Harry's voice.

I heard his steps heading for the kitchen and decided to join him. This might be a good time to talk, now that Grandma was in her room, fast asleep — I hoped.

"I thought you said you'd be home much earlier," I said.

"Sorry. The math problems turned out to be much tougher than I thought."

Harry was standing in front of the refrigerator, pouring himself a glass of milk. "Want some?" he asked, waving the carton. Before I could accept, he grinned sheepishly. "Actually, it's just about finished."

Typical. I sat down at the kitchen table and waited until he had made himself a snack of rolls and cold roast duck. While Harry munched, I told him about finding Grandma going around the neighborhood, visiting the garbage cans.

Harry simply shrugged. "So what's bothering you? The dining room sure looks a lot neater. Soon we'll be able to move the table to the middle of the room again."

"Harry! Doesn't it worry you that someone pushing seventy is going out in the pouring rain and throwing empty soap boxes in all the neighborhood garbage cans?"

He shrugged again. "It'd worry me more if the soap boxes were full."

I felt like throwing the milk carton at him. What was the use? Harry was good-natured, but he didn't go out of his way to help people. If you slipped on a banana skin and fell down right in front of him, he'd bend over and pick you up. If you fell ten feet away, too bad.

He was Grandma's favorite, and I was doing all the household chores — because that was the normal way in a traditional Chinese family. Boys had more important things to do, such as homework and preparing for their careers.

This wasn't necessarily true with all of the Chinese-Americans in Seattle. In some of the families we knew, the girls were beginning to count almost as equals. But with our family, the traditional ways were kept up more than with most, because of Grandma's influence.

"Harry," I said, "the Rock Hounds are planning another field trip next week, and I don't want to miss it. Can you stay with Grandma?"

"Gee, I don't know," he said. "Anyway, why do you want to spend so much time hounding rocks? Okay, I know you've always been fascinated by jade, but you can get better quality stone at a jewelry store."

He was right about jade, I thought bitterly. About four years ago, when Mother had been alive, she and I had watched Grandma rummage through the brilliantly embroidered silks, fur-lined jackets, gold lockets, sandalwood fans, and other fascinating objects inside her trunk.

"These are for Harry, of course," Grandma had said.

"You're not saving anything for Walter?" asked Mother. Uncle Walter was my father's younger brother, and Grandma's favorite.

"Walter has only daughters," Grandma said grimly. "I can't give him anything."

I had seen a round green object, shaped like a thin doughnut. "What's that, Grandma?"

"That's a jade bracelet," Grandma said. "Look how pure the color is. It's the best quality jade."

Fascinated, I put my hand through the bracelet. It was such a beautiful color, and the stone felt deliciously cool against my wrist.

"I suppose that's also for Harry," Mother had said.

"Of course," said Grandma. "I'm saving it for the day when Harry grows up and gets married, so he can give it to his wife."

Tears came into my eyes and I slowly pulled the bracelet off. Mother noticed my disappointment and sighed, but there was nothing she could do. The bracelet was not hers to give.

As I reluctantly handed the bracelet back to Grandma, she looked at me and her face seemed to soften. It lasted only an instant. Then her lips tightened, and she turned abruptly away to put the bracelet back in the trunk.

Now, as Harry contentedly ate his snack, he didn't notice that he had said anything to upset me. He never did.

As Grandma grows older, I thought, she's

13

bound to need more and more attention. I knew it was useless trying to get Harry to share the responsibility. At this rate, I might wind up spending all my time looking after her! I had to find help from somewhere.

I thought about our next Rock Hounds outing. I thought about Steve, and the promise of seeing him again in school and going out with him. No, I didn't intend to give up all that. There had to be some solution.

TWO

MOTHER HAD DIED two years ago from lung cancer. She didn't even smoke, and for months afterward I had raged over the bitter irony. Within a year, however, I was mostly over the pain of her death. Except for moments when I was really down, I could look at her picture and her special chair without tears welling in my eyes.

Father was only just getting over Mother's death. Maybe grown-ups took longer. Maybe I hadn't been so dependent on Mother. I had always known that she had to give most of her attention to Father and Harry, so I guess I learned to manage on my own.

I hadn't consciously known that there had

been a silent battle between Mother and Grandma, but now I remembered the times when Mother wanted to do something, and then later announced stiffly that plans had been changed — by Grandma, probably. There were occasions when Mother would suggest taking us all out to a fast-food place, but instead we'd wind up eating our usual Chinese supper with rice and four dishes.

Once in a while Mother got her way and we went to Kentucky Fried Chicken or something, but we'd have to face Grandma's disapproving glare. After Grandma had the household completely in her own hands, some things seemed a lot less tense. It occurred to me that this might change again if Father remarried.

Now, two years after Mother's death, Father was beginning to look at other women again. I finally found out why he had been so absent-minded recently. He was seriously interested in someone, and at the Northgate Shopping Mall, I discovered who she was.

Steve and I had arranged to meet at the mall. We had been dating since that night at the Rock Hounds a month ago. We had gone to a couple of movies together, and last weekend he took me to a rock concert (we just couldn't seem to get away from rocks). I insisted on paying for my ticket since it was so expensive, and Steve didn't argue. That's what I liked about him: no phony politeness. Like I said, Steve was relaxing to be with.

I got to the mall early, and I was looking at some stretch pants in a window when I heard someone calling my name.

"April! I can't believe it's you!"

A tall, slender Chinese woman was looking at me. She was dressed casually in a beautifully tailored tweed suit, and with it she wore a silk blouse I'd give an arm for. There was something familiar about her.

"You don't remember me, do you?" said the woman. "It's been years. I'm Ellen . . . Ellen Wu."

Now I remembered. "Of course! Your parents used to give me 'growing up money' every New Year. They were giving me as much as five dollars before I became too old — worse luck."

Ellen laughed. "It must be inflation. I never got more than two dollars from your grandparents."

Like us, Ellen was Mandarin-speaking Chinese, part of a subcommunity within the larger Cantonese-speaking Chinese community in

Seattle. Until we started high school, Harry and I had gone to a Saturday morning Mandarin language school.

Our parents organized an annual bazaar to help finance the school. They played bridge or mah-jongg together regularly, and exchanged boxes of moon cakes on the Mid-Autumn Festival. Best of all, on New Year's Day we kids used to get "growing up money" in little red envelopes from friends of our parents.

Ellen was almost a generation older, so she had never been a real friend, but someone rather glamorous seen at a distance. Now that I was sixteen and Ellen was — what, around thirty-five? — the gap between us had shrunk a little. But it was still a real gap and I hadn't seen her in years. Then why the hearty greeting?

Ellen glanced at her watch. "It's almost noon. If you're not busy, how about joining me for lunch? I know a new place nearby that serves bratwurst on rye rolls: solid food that puts meat on your bones." She laughed again. She could afford to, because she didn't have an extra ounce of fat on her.

Somewhat mystified, I accepted her invitation. I had plenty of time to spare before meeting Steve, and for a change Harry had promised to be home in case Grandma needed looking after.

The restaurant was one of those little places that I knew would start on a shoestring, do well for a few months, and then disappear without notice. This one featured paper tablecloths with a checked pattern, pots of real geraniums, and a menu with seven kinds of sausages and four kinds of mustard. I found out that bratwurst with a dark rye roll was just a glorified hot dog.

Ellen carefully picked out the caraway seeds from her roll. Then she looked up. "Did you know that your father and I have been going together?"

So that was it. That's why Father went out more often in the evenings, and why I had noticed an air of suppressed excitement about him.

I was a little hurt that he hadn't told me about Ellen. Father and I had always been close. While Harry was doted on by Mother and Grandma, I knew that I could always turn to Father for support.

Ellen was married, I suddenly remembered. "What about . . . what about . . ." I stopped, embarrassed.

"You mean Jack?" Ellen shrugged. "I've been divorced from Jack for almost a year now.

I knew it was a mistake almost from the first, but I didn't want to admit it because I didn't want to hear my family say, 'We told you so.' "

"Was it because he was white?" I asked.

Ellen shook her head. "That was the least of it. I think what it boiled down to was that Jack wasn't prepared for humdrum daily life or long-term commitments. We're still friends, but we could never have stayed married."

"Then why did you marry him in the first place?" I asked. My face became hot, as I realized how fresh my question was, addressed to an older person — to someone who might become my stepmother.

But Ellen wasn't offended, only thoughtful. "I got married to Jack McGrath because he was so unlike all the Chinese boys I had been dating." She smiled ruefully. "Things are probably different these days, but when I was your age, all the Chinese boys I met were so full of themselves, you know? They seemed to think that their mothers and sisters and girlfriends existed for the sole purpose of catering to them."

I immediately thought of Harry, and some of Harry's friends. "Things aren't all that different these days. I think it's because in a Chinese family — even a Chinese-American family — the sons are still more important than the daughters."

Ellen nodded. "Jack was so refreshingly different. The first time we went out on a date he suggested a movie, and I nearly fainted when he asked me what *I* wanted to see!"

I was in the middle of chewing a mouthful of my roll when I started to laugh. It was all I could do not to spray crumbs all over the table. "That's exactly what happened when I went out with Steve for the first time!" I took a drink of water. "Steve is my boyfriend, and he's a lot of fun." After a moment I added, "He's white. I haven't introduced him to my family yet."

Ellen nodded somberly. "Jack was a lot of fun, too . . ." She broke off, then looked intently at me. "Don't ever confuse fun with love."

"Does this mean my dad is not a lot of fun?" I smiled as I asked the question, but I didn't think that Ellen's comment was very flattering to Father.

Ellen looked startled. "You look so meek and shy, you had me fooled." She paused. "I had a serious crush on your father when I was a teenager, did you know that? Of course you didn't. You weren't even born yet."

Father as a heartthrob was a novel idea.

True, I was proud of his good looks. Although he was pushing fifty, he had kept his trim figure and his thick, black hair. He had the rangy build of the northern Chinese, and he was above average height even in America. But to imagine a teenage girl swooning over him? To hide my smile, I took a big bite of my sausage.

"You think it's funny," said Ellen. "But I was absolutely devastated when your father married your mother. My heart broke into a million little pieces."

We looked at each other, and both of us broke out laughing. Ellen applied more mustard to her roll and took a huge bite. Some of the mustard oozed out of the corner of her mouth.

"Did Dad ever find out about your crush on him?" I asked. I was intrigued by this glimpse of his early life.

Ellen wiped off the mustard and shook her head. "That's what attracted me to your father. Half of the Chinese girls I knew were in love with him, but he never thought of himself as God's gift to women."

Ellen's face became serious. "This time we are both adults. I know that I can never take your mother's place, but your father and I want

22

a second chance at happiness with each other. Can you give us your support?"

I squirmed with embarrassment. "Of course. You don't have to ask."

"I know how close you are to your father, so I want us to be friends."

"Of course," I repeated. Then I added, "Anyway, I want to go away to college next year. What Dad does at home is none of my business."

Ellen looked interested. "What do you want to study?"

"I'm fascinated by stones," I said. "So I want to go to a school with a good geology department. Harry says I'm better off looking for stones in a jewelry store."

"Don't listen to Harry!" said Ellen. "Hasn't he heard? These days girls can study whatever they like."

I laughed. "I don't let Harry run my life, anyway."

"You're lucky," said Ellen. "My elder brother liked to lay down the law. We fought all the time."

"I just ignore what Harry says, and he's too lazy to do much about it," I told her.

"Maybe your way is better," admitted Ellen.

She asked the waitress for the bill. We left the cafe and began to walk through the mall, looking at the shop windows without really seeing them.

I knew that Ellen taught at the university. "What do you teach, Ellen?" I asked.

We had stepped into a natural food store. She picked up a jar of mayonnaise made with canola oil. "I teach German. My real interest is German Romantic literature."

"That's a funny subject," I blurted out.

"You're just like the others!" cried Ellen with irritation. "Nobody in my department takes me seriously, so I wind up teaching all the beginning language courses."

Ellen's bitterness surprised me. "Well, I just wondered why a Chinese woman should pick German literature."

"Why should a Chinese girl pick geology?" she demanded. "Look, there have been some outstanding German scholars in the field of Chinese literature. So why is it funny for a *Chinese* to study *German* literature?"

She had a point. "I'm sorry, Ellen," I said. "We complain about people stereotyping Asian-Americans, but now I'm doing it myself." After a moment I peeked at her. "Is that another reason why you broke up with your husband?"

Ellen put back the jar of mayonnaise. "Actually, Jack's been very good about my work. He supported me when the rest of the German department felt it was bizarre."

"You're serious about your work, aren't you?"

"You bet I am. It's the only thing that matters to me. . . ." Ellen paused, and then added with a grin, "Other than your father, that is."

That remark about Father sounded uncomfortably like an afterthought. "Are you and Dad planning to get married?"

The question sounded funny the minute it left my lips, as if I were the parent, asking whether Ellen's intentions were honorable.

We turned and left the natural food store. Ellen didn't answer immediately. As we walked past a shoe store, my mind wandered and I looked wistfully at a pair of running shoes in the window. Could I afford to buy them? Maybe if I got a job this summer. . . .

"It's not that simple," said Ellen, finally breaking the silence. "When an American man and woman marry, they marry each other. When a Chinese man and woman marry, they marry each other's family as well."

I was hurt. "And you have second thoughts about marrying into the Chen family?"

Ellen was instantly apologetic. "God, I've been tactless! Look, April, by 'family' I don't mean you and your brother. You are terrific, and both of you are old enough to take care of yourselves. To be honest, what scares me is the thought of becoming a Chinese daughter-in-law. My own mother was a real terror to my brother's wife. I'm not sure I can cope with my work and your grandmother at the same time."

I had to admit that coping with Grandma took stamina. I'd had to do more and more of it recently. "Grandma is acting a bit funny," I said. "I'm wondering if we should take her to a doctor."

"Maybe she needs the full-time care of a nursing home," said Ellen. She sounded almost eager.

"I think it's too early to talk about that," I said stiffly.

Ellen grimaced. "I can't seem to say anything right today." She put her arm around my shoulder. "Forget what I said just now. The only thing to remember is that I love your father. He's different from the others."

"Different from your ex-husband or different from other Chinese men?" I asked.

"From both, I guess," answered Ellen. "I'm sure that when he marries, he marries for life.

And he doesn't act like the king of the castle at home, I bet."

"That's true," I said. It was hard to think objectively about my own father, but now that Ellen had mentioned it, I realized that Father did not automatically expect service from me. He said "thank you" when I refilled his rice bowl. Harry never said "thank you."

"Gilbert told me his brother Walter was his mother's favorite," Ellen said thoughtfully. "So maybe Walter is the one who acts like the king of the castle at home. I guess we shouldn't be in such a hurry to stereotype men — Chinese or Caucasian."

I could agree with that. "No, we shouldn't. I hate being stereotyped as a meek, studious, goody-goody Asian girl."

"And I hate being stereotyped as someone genetically incapable of understanding German Romantic literature!" said Ellen.

We smiled at each other, and I thought how great it would be to have a stepmother who could also be a friend.

"Boy, April, I've been looking all over for you!" a voice called out to me.

Steve! I had agreed to meet him in front of the record shop, and I was already late.

Steve came loping up, his eyes bright with

27

curiosity. I introduced him. "Ellen, this is Steve Daniels."

Steve stuck his hand out. It was a very big hand, and Ellen's slender fingers disappeared into his fist. "Hi. Glad to meet you." If he had a tail, he would have wagged it. I felt a moment of unreasonable jealousy. Here I was, feeling like I owned him already.

"Hello," Ellen said slowly, looking up at Steve. "I'm a friend of April's father." She was tall, but she still had to look way up. Steve was six one and still growing. Ellen glanced at her watch. "I have to run. It's later than I thought." Turning to Steve, she smiled and said, "I'm glad I met you, Steve."

Watching Ellen disappear behind a potted palm, Steve let out his breath. "Your dad sure is a lucky man."

"Don't jump to conclusions, Steve. You heard what Ellen said: she's just a friend."

"That's not what *I* heard. I heard the way she said *friend.*"

He had a point there. "Well, it's still too early to see Ellen as my future stepmother," I said. "I think she has problems with the idea of marrying into my family."

"What's wrong with your family?"

"Well, you know," I began, "you know how Grandmother is. . . ."

Steve looked away. "Actually, I *don't* know. We've been going together for a month now, and I've never been introduced to any of your family."

I didn't know how to answer him. We walked into the record shop. I followed Steve to the jazz section and started flipping through the records. After a while, I had to say something. "It's not because I'm ashamed of you, Steve. You know that."

"But I *don't* know that," Steve said again. He looked hurt. "You've met *my* folks, and they liked you, even my sister, who can be a real pain. So why can't you let me meet your family?"

I felt trapped. "Of course I'll introduce you to my family — one of these days. I promise."

Even as I spoke, I remembered the time last year when Harry had brought home a Caucasian girlfriend called Cindy. She had been a blond, bubbling kind of girl, a nonstop talker. I liked her. Harry had been very proud of her and told me that she was extremely popular in school.

Under Grandma's cold gaze, however, Cindy's stream of lighthearted chatter soon dried up. When Harry asked her to stay for dinner, Cindy had made a hurried excuse and left.

"I don't want to see you spending time with that sort of girl again," Grandma had told Harry afterward. He obeyed, of course.

Grandma had been awful about Cindy, but was it really because she was white? Maybe she just couldn't stand the nonstop chatter.

If Grandma could do this to Harry, the apple of her eye, what was she going to say to me when I brought Steve home? I could take the heat—the coldness, rather—but I refused to subject Steve to the kind of discomfort that Cindy had experienced.

I liked Steve a lot, and I wanted my family to like him too. It would be great if he and Father could become friends. I'd have to think of some less risky way to introduce him to the family—and fast.

THREE

I FINALLY THOUGHT of something. Grandma's seventieth birthday was coming up, and we were planning to give a big party for her at the Peach Garden restaurant. What if I invited Steve? Since there would be lots of guests, Grandma wouldn't have a chance to express her displeasure at his presence. This would save unpleasantness, and Steve couldn't complain anymore that I wasn't introducing him to my family.

To be honest, I had another reason for asking Steve to the birthday party. I wanted to test him out.

When I was in the second grade, I had invited a friend called Becky to our house after school. We had such a good time playing together that I wanted her to stay for supper. It was fine with my parents. Since we had plans to eat out in Chinatown, we called up Becky's parents for permission and took her along with us. The restaurant we chose was not popular with tourists and had only Chinese customers. After we had been eating for a few minutes, Becky suddenly burst into tears. It turned out that she had never been in a place where she was the only Caucasian. Being surrounded by "aliens" had sent her into a panic. It had been hard to be her friend after that.

It seemed unlikely that Steve would feel uncomfortable at Grandma's party since he was relaxed and not the nervous type. It was risky, of course, but I was curious to see how he'd react on finding himself a member of the minority for a change.

That night I was in the kitchen putting away the last of the supper dishes when Father came in to make some fresh tea. He poured me a cup and we started to chat, as we often did. I told him about the latest Rock Hounds outing. "I like the field trips, and I also like the company."

He smiled. "Any one person in particular?"

I blushed a little. Then it occurred to me that this was my chance. "As a matter of fact, there is. Can I bring him to Grandma's banquet?"

He looked surprised. "Of course. You don't have to ask."

Harry came in and overheard. He winked at me. "A new boyfriend? Is he anyone I know?"

"No, he's someone in school," I mumbled. Then I took a deep breath. "His name is Steve Daniels, and he's white."

Father looked unhappy, but all he said was, "You can bring your friend if you want to, April. After all, Harry is bringing Janet."

"I don't know, April," Harry said slowly. "Grandma might get upset if she sees a foreign devil gracing her birthday banquet."

"Grandma won't have to talk to Steve," I said. "She'll be too busy with her own friends. After all, there will be more than fifty people there."

"Yes, but forty-nine of them will be Chinese," retorted Harry. "Your friend will stick out like a hedgehog on a billiard table."

"That's all right, April," said Father. "Bring your friend." He paused for a moment. "I'm inviting Ellen Wu. She told me she saw you at the shopping mall the other day. I'm glad you two got on so well together."

I had to hide a smile. Father knew that Grandma would be unhappy about Ellen, so he was in no position to object about Steve.

"What's this about Ellen Wu?" demanded Harry, and Father started to tell him about Ellen. I had passed the first hurdle.

My next hurdle was Grandma. What would she say when she met Steve face-to-face? Although she was soft-spoken and gentle looking, she had a way of letting people know of her displeasure. Janet, Harry's current girlfriend, was a member of the Cantonese-speaking community, and Grandma would make pointed remarks about not being able to communicate with her. Harry should be glad to have Steve at the party because he would make Janet look like an insider.

OUR BANQUET for Grandma was held in a big room at the back of the Peach Garden restaurant. When Steve and I arrived, we had to pass through the front dining room to reach the banquet room. Many of the guests had already arrived and were milling about waiting to be seated at their assigned tables.

I looked around nervously and saw Grandma at the head table. She was surrounded by well-wishers, some of them friends she had known for fifty years or more. Many had come over from China in the late forties and fifties, when the Communists had taken over the country.

She was busy talking, and I was glad because that gave me an excuse for not introducing Steve to her. Okay, so I was a coward.

I brought Steve over to Father's table. "Father, this is Steve Daniels."

Father was a little stiff at first, but Ellen, who was standing next to him, winked at me and said, "I've met Steve already, at the shopping mall."

That broke the ice. Father, Ellen, and Steve exchanged a few words before Father had to go and greet other guests. I discovered that my palms were damp, and wiped them on my skirt when no one was looking.

Harry came up with his friend Janet, and I found the introductions a lot easier. Steve and Harry chatted about the chances of the Husky football team next season — with most boys, sports always filled any gap in the conversation.

Thank heavens all my immediate family were taken care of, except for Grandma. There were still Uncle Walter and his wife, but they were from out of town and could wait. Besides, people were sitting down at their tables and the banquet was beginning.

Steve and I were seated at a table of young people, and the conversation was mostly in English. Many of the Chinese-American kids I knew were more comfortable in English, even when our first language was Chinese. Steve asked the girl next to him about the various items in the dish of hors d'oeuvres, and soon the two of them were discussing barbecued pork. I stopped worrying about him.

I glanced over at Grandma's table and saw her lean over to talk to Mrs. Liang, her oldest and closest friend. She hadn't glanced at my table — so far.

In the middle of the Chinese faces, Steve's red hair and prominent nose suddenly seemed to stick out. But to give him credit, he managed his chopsticks expertly. He succeeded in picking up the slippery jellyfish from the cold hors d'oeuvres dish, which even some of the Chinese guests found difficult. Steve was not Becky, and he had no problem being a member of the minority here. I was proud of him.

Father and Uncle Walter and his wife were each acting as a host at three of the tables. If Mother had been alive, she would have served as hostess at one of the tables. I knew that Father had wanted to ask Ellen to be a hostess, but he had chickened out at the last minute. Or maybe, I thought, he had asked and she had refused, not yet willing to commit herself as a future daughter-in-law. Instead, she sat with Father while two friends from the older generation presided over the remaining tables.

At the head table was Mrs. Liang, who was preparing to give a toast. She couldn't stand up because she had broken her hip and was still in a wheelchair, but she raised her glass high and everyone else at the table followed suit.

Suddenly I remembered the toasts at Grandma's previous "round" birthday: her sixtieth, when I was six years old. As I recall, Mrs. Liang had proposed the birthday toast then, too. After everyone had raised his glass of champagne, Grandma had risen to thank the company. Her face had been flushed, and she was smiling.

She gave her thanks to the assembled guests. Then she said, "I have an announcement to make."

She waited until she had everyone's full attention. "Since the death of my husband three months ago, I have been making plans for my future. As you know, we are reborn every sixty years. This means that today I have finished one cycle of life and I am starting a second cycle. In my case, I am starting a new life in a very real sense. Today I signed the papers to sell my house, and I will make my new home with my son Gilbert and his family."

A buzz of comments had gone around the room, and then clapping broke out—at first from a few scattered individuals, then the applause gathered momentum, and soon everyone was clapping.

I had been delighted. Now Grandma could tell us stories every night! We wouldn't have to wait until she babysat for us. Mother should be happy, too, that Grandma would be staying with us, I thought. She would have company while she was cooking in the kitchen.

When the party began to break up, many of the older guests came up to Father. "It's good to know that there are still dutiful sons like you," I heard one elderly man say. "Too many of our younger generation have adopted American ways, and leave their parents to live out their old age in loneliness."

But as we were leaving the restaurant, I glanced at my parents and saw that Father's face was troubled and Mother's was grim. What was wrong? Weren't they glad that Grandma was going to live with us?

38

Later at home, I overheard my parents arguing. "Why didn't you even consult me, Gilbert?" asked Mother. "To spring it on me like that at the banquet, knowing that I wouldn't be able to say a word in front of all those people!"

"I didn't know she was going to make the announcement," Father said.

"But you did invite her to live with us, didn't you?" demanded Mother. "You invited her, without checking with me first?"

"Yes, Margaret, I did mention the possibility to her. She told me she would think about it."

"She could have gone to stay with Walter! He was always her favorite."

"Margaret, I'm the eldest son. It's my responsibility to take care of my mother when she needs me."

"And I'm the wife of the eldest son," Mother said angrily. "So I don't have any choice in the matter."

Now, ten years later, I understood that having a dominating mother-in-law at home had meant that Mother was no longer in charge. Maybe that was why she had gone back to her job as a librarian.

I saw Uncle Walter go over to the head table to toast Grandma on her seventieth birthday.

After the toast he bent down to kiss her. From the way Grandma looked up at him and put her hand on his arm, I saw with complete clarity that he was her favorite son. She never looked at Father like that.

Uncle Walter chatted for a minute with Grandma and then went over to the table where Father sat with Ellen. It was funny and a little embarrassing to see Father looking like a lovesick teenager.

Uncle Walter bent down to speak to Ellen, and soon he was laughing at something she had said. I glanced back at Grandma. She was staring at Ellen, her face wooden and expressionless.

A new course arrived at our table, and it was sea cucumber braised in oyster sauce. Steve, who had bravely tried everything up to this point, pulled back when the dish was passed to him. He stared nervously at the quivering gray mass. "Uh, I'm not sure if I can handle this."

"Sure you can," I said heartily. "You've done great so far."

Soon everybody at the table was egging him on. "How do you know you won't like it if you don't even try it?" said the girl on his other side.

Eventually, Steve got a piece of the gelatinous sea cucumber into his mouth and down his throat. "It isn't bad!" he said, looking astonished. I could see that the other guests were impressed.

"How did you get so good with chopsticks?" I asked him. "You look like you were born with a pair of silver chopsticks in your mouth."

"We eat Chinese food at home a lot because my dad likes it," he said. "He also likes Japanese food and Vietnamese food and Korean food and . . ."

"Never mind," I said. "He likes anything with soy sauce in it, right?"

Soon we were all discussing the differences between the various kinds of Asian foods. When I next looked back at Grandma's seat, it was empty.

Father came up to me. "Have you seen your grandmother? The management of the restaurant wants to present her with a Peach of Longevity."

At Grandma's birthday banquets, the Peach Garden restaurant made it a practice to present her with a huge steamed bread in the shape of a peach, which symbolized long life.

I shook my head and got up. "I'll help you look."

"What's up?" asked Steve. "Anything I can do?"

"We can't find Grandma. Don't worry, it's probably nothing. I'll be back."

I went into the ladies' room, but Grandma was not there. Father and Uncle Walter looked worried when I reported. "Is it true that Mother has been wandering a bit recently?" asked Uncle Walter.

"Yes, especially at night," said Father, then told him about the soap boxes.

Uncle Walter frowned. "That sounds quite unlike her."

"How would you know?" retorted Father. "You haven't seen her for almost two years!"

"Shouldn't you at least take her to a doctor?" asked Uncle Walter angrily. "Something might be wrong with her."

"Let's find her first," Father said tightly.

Steve came up. "Want me to help you look?"

"No, that's okay," I told him quickly. "We don't want to start a panic."

Father, Uncle Walter, and I separated. Uncle Walter said he'd try the men's room. Women, when desperate, had been known to use the men's room if the ladies' side was fully occupied.

While Father went to look up and down the

street, I said I'd search the alley behind the restaurant.

Grandma was not in the alley lifting the lids of garbage cans, thank goodness. I re-entered the restaurant, hoping that she had been found in the meantime.

On my way back to the party I had to pass through the front dining room again. I squeezed my way past a big round table, where a happy family was digging into a big platter of fried noodles. The children, ranging from toddlers to teenagers, were noisily shoveling down their piles of noodles, chicken shreds, prawns, bamboo shoots, green onions, and bean sprouts. It was probably a birthday party, since noodles were a traditional birthday dish. Like the peach, they symbolized longevity.

For a moment I almost wished I were eating at this table instead of at the formal banquet with its toasts and boring speeches. Even the older members of this family, eating more sedately, seemed to be enjoying the meal more than the guests at our banquet. I glanced at a gray-haired old lady helping herself to more noodles — *Wait a minute!*

It was Grandma! She was sitting at the table, delicately putting a sliver of bamboo shoot into her mouth. Then she put down her chopsticks to ladle more noodles on the plate of a little boy next to her. The boy stared at her for a second, then thanked her in Chinese. Grandma smiled at him.

That smile reminded me of something. I had been four, or maybe five, and I had a hard time getting a piece of noodle up from my bowl. Grandma had picked it up and put it in my mouth, and then she had smiled just like that.

A man seated on the other side of the table was looking at me, and when our eyes met, he got up and walked across to me. We retreated until we stood well away from the table.

"I believe you know that old lady," said the man.

I felt the heat burning my face. "She's my grandmother. I'm really sorry she crashed your party. You didn't tell her she's at the wrong table?"

The man grinned ruefully. "At first I thought she was my brother-in-law's guest. And he thought she was *my* guest. Even after we found out she didn't belong to our party, we didn't have the heart to say anything to her since she was enjoying herself so much. Besides, the children like her."

I reported to Father and Uncle Walter, and they eventually persuaded Grandma to return to her own table. The two of them stood back, looking thoughtful as they studied Grandma.

"She has to see a doctor!" whispered Uncle Walter. "You can't let this go on!"

"Joining that other party might be eccentric," Father said, "but it's hardly dangerous."

"What if she wandered out in the middle of the night?" asked Uncle Walter. Realizing that his voice had risen, he lowered it. "She could fall! Or get mugged!"

"So you think she should see a psychiatrist? Are you suggesting that she's losing her mind?"

Uncle Walter retreated. "Of course not. But there might be some reason—a chemical imbalance or something—that's making her act funny. You should check it out."

Father finally agreed to make an appointment for Grandma to see a doctor as soon as possible. "But it won't be easy to get her to go," he said. "You know how she hates Western doctors!"

Driving home with Steve after the banquet, I didn't know whether to be worried or relieved. He had met most of my family, and Father and Harry had both been friendly enough. When I had last seen Grandma, she had been busy accepting the Longevity Peach and congratulations from her old friends. There were so many people around her, I couldn't get close. So I had an excuse again for not introducing Steve. He seemed to understand.

I told him where I had found Grandma. "We finally persuaded her to go back to her own table, but I could see that she was having a better time with the other family."

Steve looked at me curiously. "Why is that, do you think?"

I thought about it. "Harry and I are too old now to need her care. I guess she just likes little children and wanted to be where she thought she could be useful."

Steve seemed touched. "She's a doll, your grandmother. I can hardly wait to meet her face-to-face."

I didn't say anything. Why shatter his illusion?

FOUR

*I*T WASN'T EASY persuading Grandma to go to our family clinic. "Why should I see a doctor when I feel fine?" she asked indignantly when Father first suggested making an appointment.

"Mother, you haven't had a medical checkup for almost a year," said Uncle Walter. His voice was low and soothing. "Even people who are completely well go regularly for checkups."

"Why do I have to go to a clinic with Western doctors?" demanded Grandma. "I can't understand the outlandish way they talk."

"They're just using medical terms," said Father.

"They deliberately talk like that so I won't understand them," muttered Grandma. "I'd rather go to Dr. Guo."

For years, Grandma had consulted the bearded, dignified Chinese doctor. He would feel her various pulses with his long, sensitive fingers and then give a learned discourse on her illness in classical Chinese. I noticed that Grandma never complained about not under-standing Dr. Guo. In the end, he would pre-scribe an herbal medicine, which we'd buy from a Chinese medicine shop.

"Dr. Guo retired last year," said Father. "Don't you remember?"

Grandma scowled. She hated hearing any-thing that implied her memory wasn't as good as it used to be. "Why should Dr. Guo retire? He is a perfectly fine physician!"

"He was ninety, after all!" said Father. "Why not *try* the clinic at least? That's where Harry, April, and I all go."

With help from Uncle Walter, Father finally managed to persuade Grandma to try the clin-ic — just this once.

"I'LL LET YOU OFF here while I park the car, Grandma. The parking lot is too far away for you to walk. Can you wait for me at the reception desk?"

Grandma nodded and got out of the car. Watching her walk up to the entrance of the clinic, I hoped that she understood *reception desk*.

After more than forty years in America, Grandma still spoke nothing but Chinese to us, and we were never sure exactly how much English she really understood. I suspected she understood more than she let on.

Although Father and Uncle Walter always spoke Chinese to Grandma, Harry and I sometimes resorted to English since we had trouble finding the Chinese expressions for certain things. (How do you say *cheeseburger* in Chinese?) More and more often, Harry and I would carry on a conversation with Grandma by speaking mostly in English while she spoke to us in Chinese.

"Do you think she really understood you?" I had asked once, after Harry had finished a long conversation with Grandma.

"I've never had any misunderstanding so far," he had said.

I'd have to talk to Harry one of these days about helping me with Grandma. He would have been a better choice to drive her to the clinic, anyway, since he was closer to her. In bringing Grandma today, I had to skip after-school orchestra. If I missed any more rehearsals, I might be demoted from the position of second flute to third. But it would have been out of the question to ask Harry to come home from the university in the middle of the afternoon.

When I reached the reception desk of the clinic, Grandma was not there. Had she changed her mind and decided to go home after all? I looked around, and to my relief I saw Grandma's short, chubby figure inside the gift shop near the reception desk. She was looking at some stuffed animals.

I hurried to the store. "Grandma, it's time for your appointment."

"You're too old for stuffed animals," Grandma said, sighing as she replaced a stuffed bear and reluctantly left the shop.

I gave Grandma's name to the receptionist, and we were told to take a seat in the waiting room. The magazines there were all old, and in any case, Grandma wouldn't read magazines in English.

A young nurse came out into the waiting room. "May? Is May here?" she asked, looking around the room.

When nobody answered, she looked at the card in her hand. "My?" she tried.

Still no one responded. The nurse's glance came to Grandma. "Are you May? Or My? Er . . . maybe I'm not pronouncing your name right."

I finally understood. "My grandmother's name is Mei-yun Chen. Is she the one you're looking for?"

The nurse smiled with relief. "She sure is. So I got it right the first time." She looked down at Grandma. "Come on in with me, May."

I remembered the respectful way everybody addressed Grandma at her birthday party: Grandma Chen or Auntie Chen by the younger generations, and Mrs. Chen by those of her own generation. Only very close friends, like Mrs. Liang, were allowed to call her Mei-yun. Even though Grandma was acting funny lately, she was still entitled to her dignity. It seemed disrespectful for this young nurse to address Grandma by her first name — and get it wrong, too.

"My grandmother's given name is not May," I said firmly to the nurse. "It's Mei-yun. But please call her Mrs. Chen."

The nurse continued to smile brightly. "I know you people have your own customs, but it's our policy here to use first names. We feel more comfortable with that."

The condescending way she talked really grated on me. "*You* may feel more comfortable with first names, but how do your patients feel?"

I was talking to air. The nurse was already leading Grandma down the corridor. Fuming, I got up and followed. At the door to the doctor's office, the nurse asked me to wait outside. "While your grandmother is seeing Dr. Wilton, can you fill out these forms for us? We need some information since this is her first visit."

I looked at Grandma's face, which seemed to be showing signs of panic. "I think I should go inside with her," I said. "My grandmother doesn't speak much English."

"That's all right," the nurse assured me. "She doesn't need to."

Before I could say another word, the door to the doctor's office shut in my face. I took the forms the nurse gave me and sat down on a chair in the waiting room. I knew immediately that I couldn't answer half the questions on the sheet. For a start, I didn't know her maiden name or how many siblings she had. Nor did I have a clue about her medical history.

I finally decided to fill in the answers that I knew and then ask Grandma about the rest. Just as I was putting away my ballpoint pen, the nurse came out and rushed up to me. "Can you come with me? We're having a little trouble with your grandmother."

"What's the matter?" I asked, as we hurried to the examination room.

"The only thing she'll let us do is take her blood pressure," said the nurse. "But she won't get undressed! Dr. Wilton can't examine her unless she gets undressed!"

We entered and found Grandma cowering in the far corner of the small room. Her eyes looked wild. Dr. Wilton sat back in his chair, humming a tune and pretending to look at a magazine.

He was older than Dr. O'Malley, the young family doctor that Father, Harry, and I went to. Grandma had visited Dr. O'Malley only once and had complained afterward that he tried to joke with her. "Dr. Guo always had a serious demeanor," she had said. "How can this young doctor expect to treat patients properly when he chuckles all the time?"

A friend had finally recommended Dr. Wilton, an older, more serious family practitioner.

"Don't worry, he has no sense of humor whatever," the friend had said. "You can count on it."

Dr. Wilton did not have a beard or long, sensitive fingers, but he did have a bushy, white mustache. He looked up at me with barely concealed exasperation. "Well, young lady, can you persuade your grandmother to let us examine her?"

I couldn't blame him for being irritated, but they could have avoided all this if they had let me enter the examination room in the first place. I went over to Grandma. "The doctor only wants to look at you, Grandma, to see if there's anything wrong."

Grandma clutched at her cardigan, which had the two top buttons undone, and then broke into a torrent of Chinese. Old Doctor Guo had never removed her clothes! He understood decency!

"She wants you to examine her without taking off her clothes," I said to the doctor.

This time Dr. Wilton didn't even try to hide his impatience. "My dear young lady, surely you can see that this is impossible."

I began to feel exasperated, myself. "Why is it impossible? You're going to listen to her heart, aren't you? Can't you just lift up the back of her sweater?"

"But that's not the way we do things here!" said the nurse.

"Well, why not?" I demanded.

There was a little silence. Finally the doctor sighed. "If that's the only way to get things done, we'd better humor her."

The nurse approached Grandma. "Come on, May, the doctor's not going to hurt you. He's just going to listen to your heart."

Grandma finally turned to the doctor, who looked resigned. She nodded and allowed the nurse to lift the back of her sweater and blouse.

"The doctor is going to put his stethoscope against your back, May," cooed the nurse. "It will feel a little cold. He wants to hear if there's anything wrong with your heart or lungs."

Grandma jerked when the stethoscope touched her back but made no further complaint. "Your heart is important, dear," explained the nurse. "It pumps blood through your body. And your lungs bring oxygen into your bloodstream. So it's important to know that they're all working well."

Next, Dr. Wilton looked into Grandma's eyes, ears, and throat, while the nurse continued to coo and explain the procedure.

Her tone of voice was really getting to me. Did she have to talk like that? Was Grandma as irritated as I felt? Her face showed so little expression, it was hard to tell.

"Heart and lungs sound all right," said the doctor when he had finished. "I don't see anything wrong with her eyes, ears, or throat. The major problem at the moment is her blood pressure. It's a little too high."

He turned to me. "Your grandmother should cut down on her salt—or should I say soy sauce?" He stood up. "She looks basically healthy, but we'll need a urine sample."

The doctor patted Grandma on the shoulder. "You're doing all right, May," he said slowly, loudly, and distinctly, as if to a very young child.

When the doctor left, the nurse handed me a plastic cup with a paper lid and a wad of gauze. "You can take your grandmother to the rest room down the hall."

The rest room had one commode and one washbasin, and was obviously intended to be used by only one person at a time. I held out the cup. "The nurse wants you to pee into this cup. I'll wait outside until you've finished."

Grandma looked incredulously at the cup and then back at me. "You're not serious!"

"You can do it, Grandma," I said, then fled outside to the corridor.

Time passed. Another patient came to the door of the rest room and I had to tell him that it was occupied. Becoming uneasy after about ten minutes, I knocked, then opened the door. Grandma was standing in exactly the same place, with the same bemused expression on her face.

"You have to pee into it, Grandma!" I said, trying to sound encouraging. Hearing giggles, I turned and saw a little boy standing behind me. His eyes, as black and shiny as olives, goggled at me. I closed the door of the rest room.

Another ten or fifteen minutes passed. The nurse who had taken us to Dr. Wilton returned. "How are we doing with our urine sample?"

I was beginning to feel frazzled. "I don't know about *your* sample," I muttered, "but my grandmother doesn't have any idea how to get *her* sample into the teensy little cup."

The nurse knocked and opened the door of the rest room. Grandma was standing motion-less in exactly the same place.

"Maybe you'd better demonstrate," the nurse told me. "Show her how it's done."

I looked at the tiny cup and decided that I

was not going to do any such thing. *"You* do it," I suggested. "You've had more practice."

The nurse glared at me for a moment. "Oh, all right. We haven't got all day."

She squeezed into the small room. "Let me show you how it goes, May. It's really very simple."

There were more giggles. The boy with the black eyes was back, and he had brought his mother with him. The nurse closed the door firmly.

As I waited, I noticed that more people were gathering in the corridor. I wished the spectators would go away, but the crowd only increased in size. "Give the old lady a drink of water," suggested someone. "Run the faucet," someone else said.

Finally the nurse emerged, holding the plastic cup, now filled with amber-colored liquid. She had an odd expression on her face.

"So you got Grandmother's sample?" I asked her. "Good work!"

The nurse's face turned crimson. "It's not your grandmother's sample, it's mine."

I tried not to laugh. "As you said, we haven't got all day. So how about letting us take a cup home with us? In a more relaxed atmosphere, my grandmother will do better."

The nurse looked sullen. "We don't usually like to do this, because we can't be sure the sample is actually the patient's."

"But at least we'll know it's not yours."

It was a cheap crack, and I almost regretted it. But I was relieved when we got our cup and were finally able to go home, away from all those giggles and staring eyes.

"That so-called doctor didn't know anything," Grandma said as we drove home.

"You mean Dr. Wilton, Grandma?" I asked, surprised. "He's supposed to be good. He had all sorts of certificates hanging on his wall."

Grandma sniffed. "Just pieces of paper. He didn't even know how to take my pulses. He felt only the one at the wrist. How can he find out what's wrong with me if he takes just the one pulse?"

I knew that Chinese doctors took pulses at various points in the body. I had often wondered what sort of information they got from the procedure. "Well, Western doctors use different methods for diagnosis. That's what the urine sample is supposed to be for." I suddenly giggled. "I bet it was the first time that nurse had to take her own sample!"

Although Grandma kept a straight face, I saw her lips twitch. "We gave the nurse a hard time, the two of us," she said, patting my hand.

"She deserved it. It was pretty annoying, the way she kept cooing and calling you May."

"You have to strike back when people treat you like a helpless idiot," Grandma murmured. Her eyes were bright.

I knew just how she felt. "And the way that nurse tried to tell you how your heart and lungs worked! She was ready to draw diagrams with a crayon!"

Grandma chuckled. That's when I realized she had only pretended to be a frightened old woman in the doctor's office. She had actually been enjoying herself. I admired her for refusing to let people put her down.

Soon we were both laughing. For a moment, the age gap of fifty-four years between us didn't seem so wide after all.

WHEN I CAME home from school on Monday and opened the front door, a cloud of delectable smells hit me in the face.

These days Grandma still insisted on doing most of the cooking, but she prepared simple meals — rice and a couple of stir-fried dishes of meat and vegetables. On weekends I took her to Chinatown and stocked up on a variety of Chinese convenience foods like sausages, pickled eggs, cans of vegetables already sliced and cooked, and packages of frozen steamed breads and savory pastries.

But the smells today were a sign of a major cooking effort. I was immediately worried that Grandma might be working too hard. However energetic, she was after all seventy years old. In China, seventy-year-old women were supported on both sides when they got up and tottered around, especially in the old days when they had bound feet.

There was something unfamiliar, too, about the combination of spices. Was she trying out a new dish? I could smell star anise, Sichuan pickle, and sesame oil. I had to swallow hard, because I was literally drooling.

After putting my backpack down, I turned to the living room and found a little boy there sitting on the couch, watching television.

The boy raised his head, scrambled to his feet, hurriedly turned off the TV set, and uttered a polite greeting in Chinese.

It took me a moment to remember where I had seen him before: in the Peach Garden restaurant, at the table where Grandma had invited herself. In fact, the little boy was the one she had been serving with noodles.

"How are you?" said the boy. "My name is Li Xiaobao. The old lady invited me to visit."

He looked only about eight years old, so his formality was impressive. But the "old lady" part startled me. It seemed a rather cavalier way to refer to Grandma. Then I remembered that

62

age was revered in China, and the boy was just being extremely respectful.

I managed a polite smile. "I'm very glad to see you again. Is your mother here?"

The boy nodded. "She's in the kitchen."

That explained it. Mrs. Li, the boy's mother, was helping with the cooking.

The door from the kitchen opened, sending another waft of delicious smells. Grandma entered, smiling broadly. "We're getting a feast tonight."

"I hope you haven't been working too hard, Grandma," I said.

"I haven't been working at all," said Grandma. "Mrs. Li is the one who is doing the cooking."

Mrs. Li? This was her first visit, and she had wound up slaving away in the kitchen. I could see how she had been drafted. She had probably been told that Mother had died and that Grandma did the cooking. Mrs. Li must have felt obliged to offer some help, and in no time found herself making the major part of the meal. Grandma could be awfully persuasive.

Her face softened as she looked at the little boy. "Don't you think Harry has grown?"

Harry was nowhere in sight, and he certainly hadn't grown much since Grandma had seen him that morning. She was mistaking the Li boy for my brother! Uncle Walter was right: Grandma's mind was getting confused.

Grandma turned to me and said, "Bring Harry some juice."

When I came back carrying the juice, the boy had apparently got over his shyness and was smiling back at Grandma and chatting. He didn't seem to worry about being addressed as Harry. He probably thought it was an American term of endearment.

After the boy had finished his refreshments, I brought him a picture book to amuse himself. I took some pleasure in finding him a book that had inscribed inside, "This book belongs to Harry Chen" in large, round, childish writing.

The boy was less interested in reading the English book than in studying our living room. He looked obviously impressed.

Personally I found our house rather gloomy, especially now that Grandma kept it dark by changing most of the sixty-watt bulbs to forty-watt ones. We had a wooden frame house, built in the twenties, with leaded windows in the living room. The furniture in the room consisted of a big sofa and matching chairs, covered in dark brown velvet. In the middle of the room was a dark blue Chinese rug with a border of birds and flowers. I knew it was a valuable rug, but I found it old-fashioned and often wished we could have a cheerful shag rug, like the one in my friend Judy's house.

Some of the furnishings in the room were Grandma's, brought over when she had come to live with us. They included a big carved rosewood chest, inlaid with mother-of-pearl, as well as a nesting set of carved teak end tables. Most of Grandma's belongings were valuable, but they were all made of dark, tropical wood. Even the landscape paintings hanging on the walls were all in dark or neutral colors.

"Can I do something to help with dinner, Grandma?" I asked.

"You don't have to do a thing, April," said Grandma. "Go upstairs and do your homework. I'll call you when dinner is ready."

So at least Grandma knew who *I* was.

When Father and Harry came home at dinnertime, I went down to the dining room and found Grandma seating the family around the table.

"Sit here next to me," said Grandma, beckoning to the little boy.

The boy came over promptly, glanced shyly at the others, and sat down on the chair indicated by Grandma.

The kitchen door opened and Mrs. Li came out, carrying a platter of stir-fried prawns. Her face was flushed and gleaming, and she wore the same shy smile as the little boy.

"Your mother invited me and my son for dinner," she said softly to Father. "I didn't feel it right to make her work hard, so I offered to cook a few specialties of my hometown in Anhui. I hope you'll find them edible."

Father breathed in deeply the luscious smell of prawns, ginger, wine, and scallions. "I don't have any doubts about their edibility."

"Me neither," Harry said enthusiastically. He helped himself lavishly to the prawns.

Mrs. Li's face became even redder. "I'll bring out the other dishes."

The dishes she brought out one by one were not elegant banquet food, such as roast duck or winter melon soup with shark fin. Mrs. Li had prepared the type of food eaten at home during an informal meal. Nevertheless, they must have involved painstaking labor. The pork was sliced into shreds no thicker than toothpicks and stir-fried with black mushrooms cut into paper-thin slivers.

I saw that one of the dishes was Father's favorite: Lion's Head—huge meatballs cooked with nappa cabbage until they nearly fell apart.

"I haven't had this in years!" exclaimed Father, looking delighted. "Mother hasn't prepared it lately, and it's not a dish you find in restaurants since it takes such a long time to cook."

Mrs. Li's face, already rosy from doing all the cooking, now turned an even brighter red. "I tried my best, but this must not be up to your usual standard."

"It's wonderful!" mumbled Father, talking around a meatball.

Grandma cut up a meatball and served it to the young boy. "Sit down and eat, Mrs. Li," she said. "You've worked hard enough!"

"As soon as I bring out the soup," said Mrs. Li, hurrying to the kitchen and bringing out a big tureen of sour-hot soup. She finally dropped into her chair, mopped her brow with the napkin, and picked up her chopsticks.

For a while conversation lapsed as we busied ourselves with the food, which was certainly worth the attention. After my initial hunger had been satisfied, I was able to look around at the two guests. The little boy was eating mostly rice and looked up to his mother for permission each time he helped himself from one of the dishes.

Harry, on the other hand, almost monopolized the prawn dish. Nor did he neglect the meatballs and the stir-fried pork. But like most Chinese-Americans my age, he ate only a small amount of rice. Compared to the little boy, Harry seemed somehow swinish in the way he was shoveling down prawns. I was embarrassed in front of our guests.

The Lis, however, didn't seem like guests anymore. Mrs. Li was more like the hostess since, after all, she had done the cooking. No, that was not right either. Grandma, sitting at the head of the table, was obviously the hostess. Now I understood. Mrs. Li was more like a *daughter-in-law*, anxiously serving the menfolk and her mother-in-law.

No wonder Grandma looked pleased with herself! This was the kind of family scene she wanted: a cowed, servile daughter-in-law who did all the cooking, with a sweet little boy who spoke beautiful Mandarin.

I glanced at Mrs. Li. Now that her flush had died down, her face had a delicate pallor. I thought of Ellen Wu. Ellen seemed so chic, athletic, and restless — by comparison Mrs. Li, with her work-worn hands, looked plain, even dowdy. But not restless. She was very restful to have around.

Could Ellen have cooked this elaborate dinner? Could Ellen even cook? I'd bet anything that grinding coffee and toasting a bagel were the extent of her activities in the kitchen.

Nor could I imagine Ellen rushing around to serve the family. She'd be more likely to tell Father to set the table and Harry to leave some prawns for the rest of us.

A few sharp words from a stepmother like Ellen might be good for Harry, I thought. Then I saw Father smiling happily and taking another Lion's Head meatball.

Grandma began to chat with her guest. "Don't forget that Gilbert has trouble digesting fried food," she whispered to Mrs. Li. "He's been like that since he was a boy. You should cook more stews and soups for him."

Mrs. Li blinked, and her face slowly turned red again. "I'm n-not s-sure . . ." she began to stammer.

"Also, you have to remember that he likes his rice on the soft side," continued Grandma. "So you have to use a ratio of one cup of rice to one and a half cups of water."

Mrs. Li looked so embarrassed that I felt

sorry for her. Had Father overheard? No, he was on the other side of the table, and he seemed to be busy helping himself to his favorite dish.

Harry, however, was listening with obvious enjoyment. "Hope you come back often, Mrs. Li," he said. He turned to me and winked.

I was disgusted with him. Grandma's obvious matchmaking didn't bother him at all. He didn't care who Father married, as long as he had good food served to him.

At the end of the meal I helped Mrs. Li clear the table but refused to let her wash the dishes. "We have an automatic dishwasher," I told her.

With no more work to be done, Mrs. Li prepared to leave. Socializing after eating was not part of a Chinese dinner party. She took out her bus schedule. "We can catch the seven forty-eight bus."

"I can give you a ride home," I offered. Harry, of course, was busy with a set of math problems, and Father, looking faintly guilty, said he had an engagement.

At the door the boy turned around to Grandma. "Thank you very much, Grandma Chen."

She smiled at him. "My, you're well behaved, aren't you? By the way, you can keep the book. I'm sure Harry wouldn't mind."

So Grandma had known all along that the boy was not Harry. Interesting!

In the car, conversation was difficult. I had almost exhausted my store of polite phrases in Chinese, and Mrs. Li's English was very basic. But by patchwork, we were able to exchange bits of information.

I learned that Mrs. Li was a widow who had arrived from China two weeks earlier with her son and was staying with her brother-in-law. "He has a green card and is a permanent resident," she said wistfully. "My son and I only have tourist visas, so we can't stay in this country. It would be different if we had closer relatives in America."

She looked at me. "Your mother is dead, isn't she?"

She means, "Is your father a widower?" I thought, although I couldn't really blame the woman for thinking along those lines, not after Grandma's comments about the way Father liked his rice cooked.

"Yes, my mother died a little more than two years ago," I replied. After a pause I added, "My father is thinking about remarrying. There's a woman he likes very much."

I stole a glance at my passenger. Mrs. Li sat looking down at her hands, and in the backseat, the little boy closed the picture book he had been looking at. I felt as if I had stepped on a caterpillar that might have turned into a pretty butterfly.

Mrs. Li gave me directions to her brother-in-law's apartment, and when we arrived, she got out with her little boy and both stood waving politely until I drove away. There was something forlorn about the two figures standing by the curb.

I didn't have time to dwell on Mrs. Li. I had to hurry back because Steve was coming over to take me to the movies. Besides, I had to hand the car over to Harry so he could drive to the university.

As I frantically combed my hair and changed into a better-looking sweatshirt, I suddenly realized that Mrs. Li's place was on the way to the university and Harry could easily have driven the Lis home! A month ago, such a possibility wouldn't even have occurred to me. Maybe it was Steve's influence. That night when he had first taken me home after the Rock Hounds meeting, he had asked me why Harry couldn't have stayed home with Grandma. For the first time in my life, I asked myself: why indeed?

STANDING IN FRONT of the multiplex theater, Steve and I had to decide among the various offerings: a science-fiction horror movie with self-reproducing robots, a comedy in which the toddlers stage a revolution and take over their nursery school, and a Japanese samurai movie about a wandering blind swordsman.

I liked comedies, and I was on the point of proposing that we go to the nursery school movie. Then Steve said, "Is it okay if we go to the Japanese movie? My dad was stationed in the Far East, and I've always been interested in that part of the world."

At least Steve asked if it was okay. Although I didn't like movies with subtitles, I agreed. For a moment I wondered if Steve was just interested in me because I was Asian and because his dad had been stationed in the Far East.

The movie actually turned out to be very funny. It was about a blind swordsman who tripped over every little pebble in the road. But somehow, by sound alone, he managed to defeat a whole crowd of attackers in a sword fight.

It was so incredible that we laughed until

our sides ached, and when we left the theater, our hands were dripping with popcorn oil.

Popcorn was not enough to satisfy Steve, so we wound up at McDonald's, where Steve had a Big Mac with french fries. I could only manage a regular hamburger.

Rearranging the sliced pickle in my hamburger bun, I told Steve about Mrs. Li's visit. "After Grandma told Mrs. Li how Dad liked his food cooked, the poor woman must have thought she was being welcomed into the family as a daughter-in-law."

Steve poured ketchup over his french fries like molten lava. "And there isn't any chance of that?"

I shook my head. "Dad is obviously in love with Ellen Wu. You've seen her. She's more than a match for a shy widow fresh from China, even one who is a great cook. I really feel sorry for Mrs. Li, and for her little boy, too."

Steve suddenly put his hand over mine. "That's what I like about you, April. You care about everybody: your grandmother, your dad, Ellen, and even a stranger, a poor widow from China."

When he smiled at me like that, my heart turned over. Steve did like me for myself.

I looked down at my hamburger and saw

that I had eaten my bun and pickles without realizing it, but had somehow left out the meat patty. "I like you, too, Steve," I said softly.

He grinned. "Because of my pretty face? That's okay, you don't have to answer. I was just fishing for compliments."

I looked up and smiled back. "I like you because you don't panic — even when you have to eat jellyfish with chopsticks."

It was Steve's turn to look shy. He busied himself with his french fries and then pulled at his milk shake.

He finally broke the silence. "Do you think you'll be able to go to the Rock Hounds outing next week? It will be on the Olympic Peninsula, near Hurricane Ridge."

"You bet! Nothing can stop me!" Then I added, "If I don't have to stay home with Grandma."

There was a pause. Then Steve said, "Is there something seriously wrong with your grandmother? Something you haven't mentioned?"

I stirred uncomfortably. "That's the trouble. We don't know. You saw how she went off to join another party at her birthday banquet." I told him about Grandma calling the little boy Harry. "You'd think she wanted us to believe she was getting confused in her old age. Why would she do that?"

Steve finished his milk shake with a loud slurp. "From what you said, she seemed to know the boy wasn't Harry—when it suited her."

"She certainly keeps us guessing," I sighed.

"Your grandmother may be just a little wacky," said Steve. "It's not like she's got a real health problem or anything. Have you taken her to a doctor?"

"We went last week, and the doctor couldn't find anything immediately wrong with her. . . ." I broke off and started to laugh.

"What's funny?"

So I told him about the nurse and the urine sample. Steve broke out in his big wide grin. "She's fantastic, your grandmother! I've got to meet her! Too bad I didn't get a chance at the birthday party."

"I guess she must be pretty healthy if she could pull off a trick like that," I said.

I found out that I was wrong.

SIX

I'M CALLING from Dr. Wilton's office,"
said a vaguely familiar voice. "I'm trying to
reach May Chen. Am I calling the right
number?"

The mention of "May" gave me a clue. It
was the nurse at the clinic, only she was no
longer using a cooing voice or baby talk. She
sounded desperate.

"This is Mrs. Chen's residence," I said cautiously. "Can I give her your message?"

"At last! At last!" said the nurse. "I tried
earlier, but the person who answered the phone
didn't seem to understand what I was saying."
A squeak of hysteria entered her voice. "I

couldn't even find out if she was the right Chen!"

I began to feel uneasy. "I'm Mrs. Chen's granddaughter. In fact, I'm the one who brought her to Dr. Wilton's office. What's the message?"

"Thank heavens I got you!" cried the nurse. "We got the lab report on May's — I mean, Mrs. Chen's urine sample. I'm afraid there are indications that she might be NIDDM."

My alarm increased. Why couldn't the nurse use ordinary English? "Could you explain that, please?"

"NIDDM means noninsulin-dependent, or type two diabetic."

Diabetes. My stomach lurched. "What . . . what does that mean exactly?" One of my classmates in school had it, and I knew it was a very serious condition.

The nurse's voice became brisk. "Dr. Wilton will have to see May, uh — Mrs. Chen as soon as possible. The condition could become very damaging, even life-threatening, if she isn't treated."

"But we went to the clinic weeks ago!" I protested. "It took you that long to do the tests?"

"The tests were done almost right away!"

the nurse said indignantly. "We sent a written report on the tests to Mrs. Chen's address and included a letter advising her to make an appointment with Dr. Wilton as soon as possible. She will have to prepare for a test on her plasma glucose concentration, and that means fasting the night before her appointment. All this is in the letter. When we didn't hear from her, we tried phoning her."

"Are you sure you sent the letter to the right address?" I asked. Even if Grandma had not understood the letter, Father would certainly have seen its importance.

The nurse confirmed the address. I promised to pass the message on to Father and Grandma immediately.

After hanging up, I thought, mail does get lost occasionally, and Grandma may very well have failed to understand the nurse's phone message. But it was also possible that Grandma had opened the letter from the doctor and understood its contents perfectly. Like many educated Chinese, Grandma could read English fairly well, even if she missed a great deal of the spoken language — and I was beginning to realize that she missed less than she appeared to.

Was it possible that Grandma had actually

read the letter and suppressed it? Just as she had failed to mention the telephone message?

When Father came home that evening, I told him about the nurse's call.

His eyes widened with alarm. "Oh, my God!" he said, rushing into the kitchen.

Grandma was picking the ends off some snow peas and looked up calmly. "What's wrong, Gilbert?"

"Did you see a letter from the doctor's office a week or so ago?" Father demanded.

Grandma turned back to the kitchen counter. "How do you expect me to remember the mail that came so long ago? Besides, there's so much junk mail! I just throw away anything that doesn't look like a personal letter."

That wasn't true. Grandma couldn't possibly have thrown away all the business mail that came into the house. She was lying. Or was she?

Father's face was grave. "Mother, the letter from the doctor says you might have diabetes. It's a serious matter. We have to take you to the clinic for tests."

"Very well," Grandma said calmly. But I noticed her hands were not quite steady as they went back to picking the snow peas.

Grandma had read the doctor's letter, after all.

FATHER TOOK a day off from his office in order to bring Grandma to the clinic for her blood test. While Grandma was getting her coat on, I asked Father what the test consisted of.

"The nurse said she'll give Grandma a glucose tablet," replied Father, "and then she'll take blood samples at thirty-minute intervals."

I shivered. "Do you want me to go along? It must be scary, having them stick a long needle into you and drawing out tubes of blood." I remembered having had it done once. The sight of that dark red blood — my very own blood! — filling the tube made me feel faint.

Father shook his head. "Your grandmother is tougher than you think. She lived through wartime Chongqing, through all that devastating bombing. Nothing frightens her."

Father smiled at Grandma as she came downstairs, and I could see admiration as well as affection in his eyes. He was right. Dr. Wilton and his nurse might see Grandma as a fragile old lady. I was beginning to know better.

Three days later, the results of the tests came back and confirmed Dr. Wilton's suspicion. Father went alone to the doctor's office. When he came back, his face was somber. "She has type two diabetes."

"So what does that mean, exactly?" I asked.

"It's the more common kind, the type that eighty percent of diabetics have," he said heavily. "But at least she won't need insulin injections."

I sank down on the sofa with tremendous relief. One of my greatest terrors had been the thought of having to give Grandma her injections. "Does she have to take pills?"

"Yes, we'll have to make sure she takes her medication regularly. Also, she'll have to be careful of her diet." He handed me a slim booklet. "Here's the list of instructions."

I glanced quickly at the introduction and then put the booklet carefully away in the dining room buffet. I would have to study it carefully later, but I could see already that I would have to make sure that Grandma had nourishing snacks at the proper time.

Suddenly I had a thought: Why couldn't Harry look after the snacks, just once or twice a week? All his classes at the U were in the morning, and he only stayed on campus to do his homework or to meet his friends. Couldn't he give up a couple of afternoons to look after his adoring grandmother? I'd have to talk to him about it.

"By the way, where is Grandma?" asked Father. "I'll have to tell her what Dr. Wilton said."

I looked out the dining room window. "She was in the backyard a moment ago."

She was still in the backyard. She was blowing dandelion seeds over our neighbor's lawn.

Father and I looked at each other. Then he cleared his throat. "I'd better have a talk with her." I followed him into the yard.

Our neighbor, Mr. Saunders, was standing by the fence. He was literally snarling with rage and trying to wave the dandelion seeds away, but he couldn't stop them from wafting over to his lawn.

Mr. Saunders was a fussbudget who always kept his lawn neat as a pin, and whenever the leaves from our yard landed on his property, he'd rake them up and dump them on our side. It wasn't a friendly thing to do, but none of us wanted to make an issue of it — except Grandma. Now she was getting her revenge.

Father went up to Grandma and put his hand gently on her arm. "Mother, we'd better go inside. We have to have a talk about your diabetes."

I watched the two of them walk slowly back into the house. Grandma held herself erect, and her face betrayed no sign of dismay as Father told her what Dr. Wilton had said. Father was right about Grandma. She was tough.

At dinner Father told Harry about Grandma's diabetes. "Just take care of yourself, Grandma," said Harry, smiling fondly at her. "You'll be okay."

Father frowned. "It's not enough for Grandma to take care of herself. She needs some help from the rest of us, too."

"Sure!" Harry agreed cheerfully. "We'll all pitch in to help."

After Grandma had retired, Harry announced that he had to go to the library again. Father and I went and sat down at the kitchen table, and our eyes automatically went to the backyard, where Grandma had stood blowing dandelion seeds that afternoon.

Someone had to say something, so I cleared my throat. "Can diabetes affect people's minds and make them do funny things?"

Father sighed. "I told Dr. Wilton about the soap boxes." He paused.

"What did he say?"

"He laughed!" Father's face was red. "He

said when you're seventy years old, you deserve to live a little and do what you want. If Grandma wants to stuff the neighborhood garbage cans with soap boxes, we should let her."

"Maybe we should tell him about the dandelion business."

"I think he'd just laugh harder." After a moment, Father added, "I told him what you said about Grandma mixing up Harry and the little Li boy, and I said I was afraid she might be getting senile — getting Alzheimer's disease." He was whispering.

My heart skipped a beat. "So what did Dr. Wilton say?"

"He said he didn't see any signs of it in Grandma. He said I shouldn't be in such a hurry."

"I guess old people sometimes get absentminded and confused," I murmured. "It may not mean anything."

"April, I was so ashamed!" Father cried.

I knew what he meant, and his anguish wrung my heart. "You mustn't be, Dad. We all want Grandma to get well, and we'll do our best to look after her."

Nevertheless, I shared some of Father's shame. Deep down, I had hoped that Grandma might have a serious illness, so that she would have to enter a nursing home. Father would be able to marry Ellen Wu. And I would be free.

I HAD SUCH A guilty conscience that I was determined to do my best to look after Grandma. I carefully read the instruction booklet about diabetes. Since she had to eat properly and regularly, as soon as I came home from school I made it a routine to eat a light snack with her. The stretch from lunch to dinner was too long. Besides, I suspected that Grandma ate little more than rice and pickles for lunch.

When I was in elementary school and Mother was away at work in the downtown library, it was Grandma who had prepared an after-school snack for me and Harry. Now it was my turn to prepare an afternoon snack for her.

This meant, however, that I had to come home directly from school every day and miss after-school activities. The conductor of our orchestra was not pleased when I cut several afternoon rehearsals. I found myself resenting Grandma because she was the reason I got demoted from second to third flute.

I was twelve years old when my parents bought me a new Gemeinhardt flute. I ran upstairs to my room with it and gloated. After trying a few rippling arpeggios, I looked up and saw that Grandma was standing at the door.

"I used to play the flute," she said wistfully.

"Really, Grandma?" I had not known that she was musical. "Hey, maybe we can play a few duets!"

"Well . . ." She hesitated and then went to her room. She came back holding a bamboo flute. It looked like a very primitive instrument, but when she played, a soft, haunting melody floated into the air.

Since there were no keys on the bamboo flute, a lot depended on how you held your lips, and Grandma showed me how. I tried it and found it helped me with my flute, too. We didn't play many duets because I knew only Western music and Grandma knew only Chinese tunes. I could never forget the wistful look on her face when she heard me playing my new flute, and I wondered why she had given it up.

I had no right to resent Grandma just because I missed some orchestra rehearsals. But maybe I could talk Harry into staying home at least one or two afternoons a week.

"Sure, April," he said, when I mentioned it. "Whenever I have a free afternoon, I'll be glad to stay with Grandma."

"How about tomorrow afternoon, then? I've got an orchestra rehearsal from three to five."

Harry looked regretful. "Sorry, there's a midterm coming up, and I promised to go over some problems with a bunch of the guys in my class."

"Can you stay home next Wednesday, then?" With Harry, you can't give up too easily. "That's an important rehearsal for our spring concert, and I really have to attend."

"Don't see any problem with that," he said cheerfully.

But when the day came, it turned out that he had to go to the physics lab. "Gosh, I'm terribly sorry, April," he said. "You know I'd do anything for you. But there's this equipment I need for an experiment. It's finally available, so I have to grab it before somebody else does."

I tried not to get mad at him, but I was seething inside. Missing this rehearsal could mean that I wouldn't get to play the flute solo that I had been practicing for weeks.

That night I called my friend Judy and asked her about the rehearsal. "I'm afraid the conductor gave the solo to somebody else, April," she said. "I'm awfully sorry. I know how disappointed you must be."

I tried to pretend that I didn't mind.

What got me was that each time I asked
Harry to spell me with Grandma, he always
came up with a convincing excuse. After a
while, I gave up even trying to ask him. You
couldn't argue with Harry. It was like punching
a goose-down quilt: it gave way, but you
couldn't leave an impression on it.

What I minded most was missing the field
trips with the Rock Hounds and not being able
to spend so much time with Steve. He gave me
a piece of the smoky quartz he had found during
the latest outing, but it wasn't the same as finding it myself.

If I didn't find some way soon to solve the
problem of Grandma, I would have to give up
everything that mattered to me.

SEVEN

*Y*OUR BROTHER Harry doesn't have to go to classes every day, does he?" asked Steve. "Doesn't he help out with your grandmother at all?"

We were making our way through the Northgate Shopping Mall. The only time Harry was willing to spell me with Grandma was when I told him I was going to the mall.

Lately I was beginning to find Steve a great support. In the past, I would have taken it for granted that Harry's studies at the university were so important that he couldn't take the time out to come home during the day. In fact, as Harry had pointed out several times, he was already sacrificing himself by choosing to live at home and going to a less expensive state university. He could have gone to an expensive private college on the East Coast, where he had been accepted.

But in recent months, Steve had been "raising my consciousness," as he called it. He did it when I told him about Harry's Great Sacrifice. "Big deal. I bet he's just staying at home because he knows he can't get the same kind of soft treatment at a dorm."

"You think he'd miss Chinese food?" I asked.

"Not only that. What he'll miss is being the center of the universe. From what you've told me, he's had his mother and his grandmother putting him first all these years. It'd be hard to go to an exclusive school, where many of the other guys are *also* used to being the center of the universe."

"And you think Harry knows this?"

"Sure he does. Harry's not so dumb. Lazy maybe, but not dumb."

It warmed my heart to hear Steve's words. I *really* have to bring him home, I thought. But not today, not right now. I was still concerned that Grandma would disapprove, and I didn't want to upset her.

Nevertheless, I was beginning to agree with

Steve about Harry, although I still didn't dare say so at home. Father was the only one who gave me any support, but he had been brought up in the Chinese tradition of considering boys to be more important than girls. He might sympathize with me, but he wouldn't tell Harry to help me with Grandma if it interfered with Harry's studies.

Steve was also supportive about my plans to go away to college.

"I want to study geology, and my dad says that I should apply to the Colorado School of Mines," I told him.

He whistled. "Colorado! I bet you'd love it out there. Mr. Cappelli says the Rockies are a lot older than the Cascades here in the Northwest."

"Do you think you might go to Colorado, too?" I asked, suddenly realizing that Colorado was more than a thousand miles away — halfway across the country, almost.

Steve shook his head. "Maybe I won't even go to college right after graduation."

We stopped in front of a travel agency and Steve stared wistfully at the colorful posters. "If I can save up enough money, I might travel a bit in the Far East."

I felt a heavy lump in my chest at the thought

that Steve and I might separate after high school. "I'll miss you," I said and found that my voice was husky.

Steve put his arm around me. "I'll miss you, too." Then he gave me a little shake. "Hey, we sound like an installment of a daytime soap. I don't plan on traveling around forever!"

"And I won't be in Colorado for the rest of my life, either."

What I didn't say was that I might not even go away to Colorado. If Grandma's condition got worse, I might have to stay home.

WHEN SCHOOL let out in June, most of my friends looked for summer jobs. Judy, who was also a Rock Hound, had a job as a camp counselor on the Olympic Peninsula. I ached with envy when I thought of Judy hunting for agates on the beaches during her free time.

Steve was working at Wendy's Hamburgers, and he asked me if I wanted a job there, too. "Just think: We could spend the whole day together! Of course, I wouldn't be able to say much to you except 'Two cheeseburgers, hold the mayo,' but at least I could look at you over the hot fat."

"Since you put it that way," I told him, "how can I resist?"

When I mentioned Steve's suggestion at dinner, Grandma frowned. "Why should a daughter of the Chen family work in a restaurant? Are we too poor to feed you properly or buy you decent clothes?"

Harry was supportive at first, in his condescending way. "April might enjoy earning a little money herself. Lots of my friends do it."

Father didn't raise any objections at the table, but he spoke to me afterward, when we were alone in the living room. "If you're out working most of the day, who will look after Grandma?"

I had thought of this already. "It's summer vacation, so Harry can be with her. He keeps saying that he should spend more time with Grandma, and now he has his chance."

When I suggested this to Harry, he said, "You know how much I'd like to, but I signed up for this intensive summer school course, and it's going to take up all my time."

I was crushed, but there was nothing I could say. Father would agree that Harry's classes were important — certainly more important than my earning some pocket money.

Steve was puzzled when I told him. We were meeting again at the shopping mall. "If Harry is so busy going to summer school, how

94

come he always finds the time to stay with Grandma when you come here?" he asked.

"Harry thinks that going to a shopping mall is a legitimate reason for a girl to leave the house," I said bitterly. "He's willing to watch over Grandma and give me a break. He says he knows how much girls love to shop."

We sat down on a bench surrounded by plastic rubber plants (rubber plastic plants?), which decorated the main walk of the mall. Steve chewed his knuckles while he thought. "Let me see if I've got this straight. Harry won't put himself out so you can earn money. But he will if you're going window-shopping."

"That's right." I was used to Harry's ways, but now I saw how things looked through Steve's eyes. "Earning money is supposed to be unimportant — at least that's what we're taught."

Steve leaned back against the bench. He looked totally relaxed, and the only sign of mental activity was the knuckle-chewing. "Well, I was taught differently," he said finally. "In my family, earning money is important. It's supposed to give you a sense of independence and responsibility."

"I guess we must seem awfully weird, then."

I glanced at him. "Do you think we're weird?"

"No. It's just that your customs are different."

I looked at him again and decided he meant what he said. One of the things I liked best about Steve was that he was curious and nonjudgmental about different peoples and different customs. "A stack of *National Geographic*s must have fallen on my mom when she was pregnant with me," he had explained.

"You can always get a job and pretend you're going window-shopping every day from nine to five," Steve finally suggested with a smile.

It sounded like such a good idea that I almost agreed.

Every outing with Steve involved stopping for a snack, and this time we wound up at the Godfather's Pizza parlor. "Let's get the Family Feast special," suggested Steve.

I looked at the description of the special: a large pizza, a dessert pizza (with sugar and cinnamon instead of cheese), and a plate of bread sticks. "You're crazy, Steve! This is for a whole family, not two people!"

"Come on, April, I'm treating."

I finally managed to talk him into getting just one pizza, giant size. When eating pizza,

Steve's trick was to put two slices together, with the gooey sides sticking to each other. "This way I don't burn myself on the hot cheese," he explained.

I tore my fascinated gaze from Steve's pizza "sandwich" and picked at a piece of pepperoni on my own slice. "You know, I sometimes think my problems would be solved if Dad married Mrs. Li, after all. She would take good care of Grandma, and I could go off to college without a worry."

Steve stopped chomping for a moment. "Didn't you say that's what your grandmother was working on?"

I nodded. "She doesn't want Dad to marry Ellen Wu, so she's looking for a way to sabotage that. And one way is to turn Dad's attention to Mrs. Li."

Steve slapped two more pieces of pizza together. "I can't believe your grandmother is such a schemer. Of course, I only saw her from a distance at the birthday banquet." He suddenly looked up at me. "When do I finally get to meet her?"

I couldn't meet his eyes. "Soon, I promise. Grandma needs a little time to get used to the idea of — of . . ." I added in a rush, "It's not because I'm ashamed of you, Steve."

"So why can't you let me meet your grandmother?"

I took a deep breath. "I don't think she likes to see me going out with a Caucasian boy. When Harry brought his girlfriend Cindy home, Grandma made it very clear she didn't approve because she was Caucasian. And Harry is the apple of her eye."

Steve stared at the slice of pizza in his hand. "Why do you care so much what your grandmother thinks? I mean, *my* grandma is a sweet old lady. We have her over every Thanksgiving and Christmas, and she's given us some really neat presents. But that doesn't mean she gets to pick my girlfriends."

I tried to make him understand. "It's different with me. I've been brought up to respect my elders, and doing something to displease my grandmother feels almost as bad as breaking a law."

"Sounds like you're scared to death of your grandmother."

"No, I'm not!" I protested. But even as I said it, I realized that I hadn't been completely honest. "Okay, maybe a little scared. Even Harry is. He broke up with Cindy because of Grandma, and I don't want that to happen to us."

Steve smiled at me. "It won't happen. Harry may have bigger biceps, but you're tougher."

"I guess I am," I said slowly and suddenly felt much better. "You know, I suspect Grandma respects toughness. She's always telling us stories about strong women in Chinese history. They're not called Dragon Ladies for nothing! Grandma's role model is Wu Zetian of the Tang Dynasty. When her husband the emperor died, she outmaneuvered a whole bunch of generals and ministers and made herself the ruling empress!"

Steve nodded. "Yeah, my dad knew gruesome stories about that dowager empress — you know, the one who was in the movie, *The Last Emperor*."

He took a big bite from his pizza and chewed thoughtfully for a minute. "You're not missing orchestra rehearsals and Rock Hound meetings just because you're scared of your grandma, April. She may be a Dragon Lady, but you must also admire her, don't you?"

That was true. "She's brave. Dad's told me stories about her courage during the war. Once when I was a kid, a huge dog came after me, barking and growling, bared teeth — it was terrifying. She stepped between me and the dog and drove it away."

"So you feel you owe her."

I nodded. "She's been living with us for the last ten years, and she practically brought us up. Since my mom had a job, Grandma took care of us when we were sick. She told us stories and read to us. She gave us a snack when we came home from school every day, and she was the one who helped us with our homework."

"You were lucky, then," Steve said gently. He grinned. "My mom's terrible at math, and after kindergarten she gave up trying to help us with our homework."

"Grandma's good at math," I said. "You know, she taught us the multiplication table in Chinese. It's much shorter and easier to remember than the one in English. Even now, Harry and I still multiply in Chinese."

"No kidding? Hey, can you teach me to multiply in Chinese, too?"

So I tried to teach him, and the rest of the pizza got cold and hard. Steve was a fast learner, but I had to teach him the Chinese numbers first. He knew some of them already from his father, who had learned them while serving overseas. Steve's tones were all wrong, and I soon broke down laughing. But I was impressed at how eager he was to learn something new.

Steve finally gave up. "Okay, I can see I'll have to stick with the English multiplication table. It's a good thing I have a calculator."

Maybe I was wrong to think that bringing Steve home would upset Grandma. How would I ever know unless I tried it?

EIGHT

I PROMISED MYSELF that I was going to bring Steve home whether it bothered Grandma or not. The trouble was, every time I came close to it, I always found some reason for putting it off. The matter was finally taken out of my hands.

On Saturday mornings, I usually drove Grandma to Chinatown to shop in one of its large Asian supermarkets. I really enjoyed the colorful aisles filled with canned, dried, and frozen foods from almost every country in Asia. The variety seemed infinite: fresh mangoes from Malaysia, dainty little Japanese eggplants, fermented Chinese bean curd, green papaya from Thailand, fish sauce from Indonesia. . . .

Grandma headed straight for the fresh food section of the store, while I wandered dreamily down the aisles of snack foods. I inspected shelf after shelf of rice crackers. Decision was hard.

"I'd go for the one over there that's ginger-flavored," said a familiar voice behind me.

I spun around and saw Steve. "What are you doing here?"

His eyebrows rose. "There's no law against white folks shopping here, is there?"

"Of course not," I said. I glanced over quickly at the fresh food section, but Grandma was out of sight. If we couldn't see her, she probably couldn't see us.

"I want to get my dad a birthday present," explained Steve. "He loves Oriental curios, but I'm not sure I can afford to buy anything here. Got any ideas?"

We went upstairs to the gift department. Since Steve's father had been stationed in the Orient, he probably knew more about that part of the world than I did.

"How long was your father in the Far East?" I asked, as we looked through some racks of T-shirts printed with the faces of teeth-gnashing, cross-eyed samurai warriors. They reminded me of the weird movie we had seen about the blind swordsman.

"He was stationed in Okinawa for three years," replied Steve. "Then he went to the Philippines to help organize some training programs."

Steve didn't think his father would go for the T-shirts, so we started looking through some cotton jackets.

"But your father is home now, isn't he?" I asked. "Would you have to live abroad if he was sent overseas again?"

"Oh, Dad's been retired for a while. He teaches history now at Seattle Central Community College."

"That's great!" I was glad, because that meant Steve wouldn't have to live the life of an army brat.

Steve winced when he saw the price tag of a judo jacket. "Actually, I wouldn't mind racketing around the world with Dad."

"Yes," I said without thinking, "but being a teacher is so much better."

Steve hung the jacket back on the rack and turned slowly to look at me. "Dad was a career officer in the army. What's wrong with being a soldier?"

"Nothing, I guess," I said. I began to realize that what I had said sounded rude, but it was too late to take back my words. "It's just that in China, being a teacher is so much more admirable than being a soldier."

"Things are different here," Steve said shortly. "In America, being a soldier is a very honorable profession."

"I'm sorry, Steve," I said. I hadn't expected Steve — who was so tolerant — to be offended. "I was taught that scholars are on the very top of the social scale and soldiers at the bottom. I didn't mean to insult your father."

"Dad wasn't thinking about the social scale," Steve said coldly. "He didn't join the army because he couldn't find a job. He did it because he thought that was the best way to serve his country."

In silence, we looked over some cloth shoes from China. I had always thought of myself as American as everybody else. Okay, I might look different from the majority of the kids, but we thought alike and we cherished the same values. I pledged allegiance to the flag with complete sincerity, and when foreigners criticized us — us Americans — I felt offended.

So it came as a shock to discover that some of my values were not the same as Steve's. "I must have absorbed my Chinese attitudes without realizing it," I said in a low voice. "Maybe it's because of having Grandma living with us."

Steve suddenly turned and looked at me. "I admire my Dad so much — I hate to hear anybody putting him down. I forgot you were brought up differently. *I'm* the one who should be sorry."

I felt a rush of affection and gratitude. Even when he didn't agree with me, he was ready to respect my different upbringing.

"April, has it occurred to you that customs and values might have changed?" asked Steve. "Even in China?"

"Well, even if they did, Grandma would never change."

That reminded me. "Oh my gosh! Grandma must have finished shopping. She's probably waiting for me to take her home!"

We went back down to the fresh food section of the store, but there was no sign of Grandma. It had been more than two hours since breakfast, and she was supposed to eat something by now. There was no help for it. Steve was going to meet Grandma whether I was ready for it or not.

Suddenly Steve began to laugh. "That's her, isn't it? Behind the fish counter?"

Behind the fish counter? Steve was absolutely right. Grandma was standing next to the sink in the back of the fish counter, arguing with the man who was cleaning fish.

"You cut off my head!" she cried. "I told you many times: don't cut off my head!"

She was speaking English for a change. The fish man was Japanese and understood not a word of Chinese. In the years Grandma had been shopping in the store, she'd always had to speak English when she explained how she wanted her fish cleaned. She wanted it scaled, gutted, but with the head and fins left on.

The fish man usually remembered, but today, apparently, he had just cleaned a pile of salmon for another customer who wanted her fish filleted. When he got to Grandma's carp, he automatically cut the head off and started to fillet it.

"Okay, okay, okay," said the fish man, throwing away the headless carp and picking up another one. His shiny head was totally bald, and he was probably as old as Grandma, maybe even older.

When he saw me, he winked. "Your grandma and I, we're old friends."

"Honestly, Grandma," I said. "You didn't have to shout at the man."

"He should have remembered that I keep my head," she said.

The fish man winked at me again. "Don't worry. We had to be quiet when we were children, so when we get old, we earn the right to shout a little."

When the cleaned fish was wrapped and handed over to Grandma, she picked it up with shaky hands. She was pale. I suddenly felt guilty. "I'd better take you home right away." I turned to Steve. "I've got to run."

He looked concerned. "Say, why don't we go to the little coffee shop here and get something to eat? Your grandmother can use some food right now."

Grandma frowned at Steve, but she was too weak to resist as we guided her to the end of the store, where there was a snack counter with some tables and chairs.

Remembering Dr. Wilton's recommendations, I ordered tea and a Chinese-style steamed bread stuffed with barbecued pork for Grandma. Steve and I had coffee.

Grandma sat down and ate her snack meekly enough. She recovered her spirit, however, after the food had given her strength. She peered at Steve for a moment and turned to me.

"Who is this foreign devil? You seem to know him."

I had been afraid of this. "Foreign devil" is what the Chinese customarily call a Caucasian, even in America. The introduction was turning out just as embarrassing as I had thought it would be. At least Steve didn't understand Chinese.

But he seemed to understand the intention, if not the literal meaning of Grandma's question. "She wants to know why you're going around with a Long-Nose, right?" He smiled as he asked the question, but that didn't make me feel better.

I refused to let Grandma spoil things. "Grandma," I said firmly, "this is Steve Daniels. He's a good friend of mine. Both Dad and Harry met him at your birthday party, but you were too busy."

"He's got spots on his face," stated Grandma, ignoring him.

"They're just freckles, Grandma," I protested. "You've seen people with freckles before. Fair-skinned people often have them."

"Yes, but we don't have to make them our friends," Grandma responded.

I suddenly realized what Grandma was: a

racist. But I didn't know the Chinese word for *racist,* and I wondered if there even was one. I also suspected that Grandma was enjoying herself at my expense. "I can make friends with freckled, foreign devils if I want," I muttered.

"Are you really that desperate?" demanded Grandma. "Why can't you ask Harry to find someone suitable for you then?"

"I don't want one of Harry's friends!"

Grandma looked surprised at my outburst. "What's wrong with Harry's friends? They all come from good families. We know who their parents are."

Of course, Steve couldn't understand a word of our Chinese conversation, but he was catching the drift. To my great relief, he didn't look offended. If anything, he seemed to be amused by Grandma's feisty spirit.

He stood and gathered up the dirty cups and plates. "I'd better go. I still have to get that birthday present for my dad. See you later, April."

I smiled at him, and as I watched him walk away with the dishes, I felt angry and relieved. Angry because I knew Grandma was trying to drive Steve away. Relieved because I had introduced him to her at last, and now he knew why I was so reluctant to do it.

I turned back to Grandma. "Harry's friends are all just like him: They expect me to wait on them hand and foot. Steve doesn't."

Grandma stared at Steve carrying away the tray. "The kind of man who doesn't expect a woman to wait on him will turn out to be unreliable. He doesn't need her. So he will be quick to desert her."

I was shocked. "That's terrible, Grandma!" Grandma was not only a racist; she was also a sexist. I didn't think there was a Chinese word for that, either. "American men simply have more respect for women. They don't expect them to act like slaves."

"White men only pretend to respect women," sneered Grandma. "But in reality, many of them prefer Asian women because they find them submissive. Look at Ellen Wu. She married a white man, but she was too stupid to hide her strong will. Her husband divorced her as soon as he found out that she didn't take orders."

I thought back to what Ellen had said about her former husband, Jack — he was charming and let her choose the movie when they went out. But he didn't want to stay married.

"That's why the divorce rate is so high in America," Grandma said triumphantly. "A stable marriage depends on mutual need, not mutual respect. So when you marry, you must look for someone who needs you, not someone who is fun."

"Is that why you brought up Harry to expect service from women?" I asked. "You want him to be dependent?"

"Of course," said Grandma. "Don't forget what I told you about yin and yang. Yin is secret and dark and feminine, while yang is open and light and masculine."

"You mean women are yin, and therefore they have to work in the dark, while men, being yang, can afford to be frank and work in the open?"

Grandma nodded. "Since we women are physically weaker, we can't overcome the men by force. We let the men see us as submissive and obedient, while all the time we control them by making them dependent on us."

"I think it's low, resorting to that kind of sneaky behavior!" I protested indignantly. I realized then that Grandma and I belonged to two entirely different worlds.

"You only say that because you've been influenced by American ideas!"

"Naturally, since I'm an American!" I retorted. "Don't forget that I was born here."

Only a few minutes ago, in talking with Steve, I had seen how different my ideas were from his. Now I realized how American in thought I really was.

Grandma's eyes flashed. "Then you will suffer all the American social problems — lack of commitment and divorce."

"It's much too soon for me to think about long-term commitments or making some poor guy dependent on me," I said, getting up.

"It's better to think of it too soon than too late," retorted Grandma.

I knew perfectly well that Grandma had lectured me because she didn't want me to have a Caucasian boyfriend. Even though I was determined not to let myself be manipulated by her, her words ate into me like acid. Every time I looked in the mirror, I could see how different I looked from Judy — from most of the girls in my class. I had heard that some Chinese girls had their eyes altered surgically to make them more Caucasian-looking. The whole idea revolted me, but I understood why they did it.

Did Steve like me just because I was Asian and he was attracted to the Far East? Did he think I was "submissive"? Would he stay faithful once my "novelty" had worn off? I had missed a couple of the recent Rock Hounds field trips, and Steve had been partnered with Judy during their outings. I wondered if Steve would eventually throw me over and go steady with Judy because she was of his own race.

The problem was that I belonged neither to the world of Steve and Judy, nor to Grandma's world. Belonging to an ethnic group wasn't as simple as belonging to the Rock Hounds. I was a minority of one, and I felt very lonely.

NINE

*I*T WAS OUR family custom to go for a picnic on Mount Rainier in early August, when the alpine flowers were in full bloom and the mountain meadows were at their best. Even after Mother died, we continued to go.

I decided to let Steve get his first heavy dose of the Chen family by asking him along for the Mount Rainier outing. We'd be forced to be together for a whole day, and he would see us at our best. Unfortunately, he also saw us at our worst.

Of course, I was taking a chance. I hadn't forgotten the rude way Grandma had treated Steve at the coffee shop, but I was optimistic about Steve. Even though Grandma had done her best to be offensive, he had taken it with good humor. A whole day of Grandma's offensiveness might be harder to take, though, especially when we'd be forced together in the car.

Father changed the scenario. Looking a little embarrassed, he took me aside the night before the picnic. "Do you think you or Harry can drive Grandma? I won't be going with you."

"You're not going on the picnic, Dad?" I asked, disappointed. Did this mean the end of the family Mount Rainier trips?

"Of course, I am going on the picnic! You know how much we all look forward to it every year!" He paused and then said in a rush, "The thing is, I'm going with Ellen, in her car."

So that was why he looked embarrassed. The trip to Mount Rainier was a drive of almost ninety miles. It would seem like nine hundred miles, with Grandma and Ellen and Steve in the same car.

For an instant, it occurred to me that we'd have a lot less stress if Mrs. Li, not Ellen, were coming along. Then I realized that just as I was making a statement by inviting Steve, Father was also making a statement by going with Ellen. He deserved my support.

"Sure, Dad, we'll be glad to drive Grandma in our car," I said quickly. Then I seized the moment. "Can Steve go on the picnic, too?"

Father knew he was in no position to protest. "Okay, as long as Grandma doesn't object."

"Steve's good at handling people," I said, trying to sound confident.

Still, I was so nervous about the picnic that I tossed and turned most of the night. When I got up next morning, I looked blearily at the blue sky and wondered what I could expect.

STEVE DIDN'T let me down. We were putting the picnic hampers in the car when he showed up. Grandma stared.

My heart was pounding, but I tried to keep my voice casual. "Grandma, Steve is coming with us to Mount Rainier today."

"You mean this foreign devil is going to spend the whole day with us?" she demanded.

Steve just grinned at her. "Sure, if you're saying what I think you are."

Grandma stared at him for an instant longer, then nodded curtly and climbed into the front seat of the car.

I nearly collapsed with relief. Harry gave me a thumbs-up sign. "You did it!" he whispered. "I didn't think you'd bring it off. Congratulations!"

"I think Grandma respects firmness," I whispered back.

"If I had known, I would have brought Janet along," he muttered.

We finished packing the car and set off immediately. Father and Ellen were meeting us at the Paradise Park picnic area at noon, and there was no time to waste.

Grandma was completely silent during the drive. Was she sulking because Father was going with Ellen? Or was it because she was forced to sit in the same car with a foreign devil? She'll cheer up when we reach the park, I thought. She loved the mountain and looked forward to the annual trip.

Just before we came to the town of Puyallup, Mount Rainier suddenly loomed up in view. The glistening white cone, standing with lonely arrogance, made everything else seem trivial. Harry pulled over into a lay-by, and for a while we all stared silently at the majestic sight.

"Chinese consider certain mountains to be

holy," I told Steve. "If Mount Rainier were situated in China, millions of pilgrims would be climbing it every year."

"I've been looking at that mountain since I was a kid," Steve said slowly. "Now I'm really seeing it." He smiled at me. "Thanks for asking me to come along."

Grandma turned around. Her eyebrows rose. She was probably surprised that a foreign devil had the sensitivity to appreciate a mountain.

Harry started the engine. "Okay, folks, now we head for the hills."

We arrived at Paradise Park fifteen minutes after twelve, and I saw that Father and Ellen had found a picnic table. They even had some food on the table already.

Ellen smiled at Grandma, but the smile looked strained. *Nin hao?"* she asked politely, which meant, "Are you in good health?"

At Ellen's greeting, Grandma nodded curtly but didn't reply. Silently, we all began to unload the hampers and set out the food.

We had brought our usual picnic treats: a roasted chicken chopped into bite-size pieces and onion pancakes — a northern Chinese dish. We also had Grandma's specialty, her home-made pickles, which she still prepared even when she no longer cooked other ambitious dishes.

As Grandma took the plastic wrap off her dish, she glanced over at Ellen, as if to say, "Top that, if you can."

"How lovely!" Ellen exclaimed, looking at the dish of salted green nappa cabbage, with slivers of yellow and red bell peppers. "Your pickles are famous among the local Chinese!" she said warmly. "I'm so glad to be able to taste them at last!"

Then she began to unwrap her own offerings, several boxes of dim sum pastries. From the lettering on the pink paper cartons, I recognized them as coming from a restaurant in Chinatown.

"I'm afraid I'm only bringing some ready-made stuff," Ellen said apologetically. "Convenience food, they call them these days."

Since the pastries consisted of shrimp dumplings, buns stuffed with barbecued pork, and steamed *jiaozi*, I thought that Ellen's apology sounded a bit unnecessary. Perhaps nervousness was making her so gushy.

"Come on, everybody," Father said heartily, "let's dive in."

With appetites sharpened by the fresh

mountain air, we needed no encouragement. We gobbled up the chicken, praised the pickles, and popped the pieces of dim sum into our mouths. After a while, even Grandma tried one of the shrimp dumplings.

Maybe the picnic will turn out to be a success after all, I thought. Maybe this will be the start of a new relationship between Grandma and Ellen.

My main worry was how Grandma and Steve were getting along. He was seated next to her, but so far he hadn't tried to strike up a conversation. He did take a big helping of the pickles and smiled at her in appreciation. I thought I saw a crack in Grandma's glacial expression. In geological terms, the crack was infinitesimal, but it was there.

Harry asked Steve about his plans for after high school.

"I'd like to travel a little before starting college," Steve said. "I'm trying to save up some money working at Wendy's Hamburgers this summer."

"Gee, I'd love to do something like that," said Harry. He sounded wistful.

"So would I," I muttered. Only I can't, because you won't help me with Grandma, I added to myself.

"By next June I hope to have enough for a couple of months in Japan," said Steve.

"Isn't Japan awfully expensive?" asked Harry.

"You're not kidding! If I didn't eat, I could save quite a bit. Beef costs around $25 a pound."

Harry whistled. "I see what you mean. Can you really go two months without food?"

We tried to think of ways Steve could avoid buying food in Japan. "You can fill your knapsack with a two-month supply of freeze-dried stuff," suggested Father. "They weigh almost nothing, and all you need to do is add hot water."

"Yes, but can you afford Japanese hot water?" I asked Steve.

He laughed. "Maybe I can go on an eating binge before I leave and store up enough body fat to keep me going."

"And if you store the fat in the right place," added Harry, "you can save money on train fare by getting tickets for the hard wooden seats."

I relaxed as I listened to the kidding between Steve and my family. He was getting along just fine, and my worries had been needless. Even Grandma had stopped looking daggers at him.

On Grandma's other side, Harry was sitting

as a buffer between her and Ellen. When Ellen found out that he was a freshman at the university, she asked him about his interests.

"Haven't decided yet," he said lazily. "I've got another year or two before I have to make up my mind. Got any suggestions?"

Ellen took that as a challenge and started listing all the reasons why Harry should go into her own specialty, German studies.

"The Chinese name for Germany is De Guo, the Country of Virtue and Morality," she began. "Furthermore—and this is crucial—the Chinese and the Germans both eat noodle soup!"

Part of Ellen's charm was that she could laugh at herself. I watched Harry being won over, and soon we were all contributing reasons for Harry to major in German.

"Just think," I said, "next time somebody sneezes, you'll be able to say *Gesundheit* with exactly the right accent."

The food had disappeared, and I began to gather up the empty plates. I noticed that Grandma's plate had an uneaten piece of dim sum. "Are you through, Grandma?"

Grandma nodded and pushed her plate away.

"Hey, don't throw that away!" cried Harry,

snatching up the morsel before I could take the plate to the trash can. He turned to Ellen. "That dim sum you brought was great!"

I glanced down at Grandma. She had been completely silent during all the laughing and joking. In fact, she had said less than half a dozen words since leaving home. Maybe she just didn't feel like taking part in an English conversation, but I suspected that she was not enjoying the picnic very much.

In the past, while the younger people hiked along some of the nature trails, Grandma spent her time in the visitors' center, which had video shows, nature exhibits, and a gift shop.

This time, there was an awkward moment after we had cleared the table. We all stood and looked at one another, wondering whether it was completely safe to leave Grandma alone on the mountain for a couple of hours.

I turned to Steve. "I'd better stay behind with Grandma. Why don't you go on the hike with the others?"

"I'll stay here with you, April," Steve said quickly.

Harry looked around at the company. His eyes rested on Grandma, whose face was stony. He seemed to come to a decision. "Dad and Ellen probably want to go off on their own, and this is Steve's first picnic with us on Rainier. I'll stay with Grandma, April."

The offer from Harry was so unexpected that for a second I just stared at him. Well, if he wanted to make up to Grandma, he should have his chance. "Okay, Harry," I said quickly. "Thanks a million."

Steve and I started for the trail before Harry could change his mind and weasel out of his offer. We soon separated from Father and Ellen, who said they wanted to go on a shorter hike and look mainly at flowers.

Steve smiled as Father and Ellen disappeared behind some subalpine firs, which were twisted and stunted by the high altitude. "We ought to let them have their privacy."

"It's a strange feeling, seeing your own father behaving like a teenager in love," I muttered.

"There's no law that says only teenagers are allowed to fall in love," said Steve. He glanced at me. "We can use some privacy, too."

We took the trail for the Nisqually Glacier. Steve said he had seen the glacier only once, and that was years ago. We didn't come across any really interesting rocks, and we didn't expect to. Mount Rainier is not a dead volcano, although it has not erupted recently, like its sister mountain, Saint Helens. What we saw were mostly dark andesites, young volcanic rocks thrown up within the last million years.

Steve loped along unhurriedly on his long legs, and I felt like a little Pekingese trotting beside an Afghan—which was only right, I thought, since my folks came from Peking, or Beijing, as people say these days.

We eventually came to places where snow still covered parts of the trail. I stopped to admire some avalanche lilies. I loved the way they poked straight out of the snow.

Steve stooped down to scoop up some snow and started packing snowballs. I looked at him suspiciously. "Don't even think of it," I said.

"Think of what?"

"Whatever it is you're planning."

"It's a basic human instinct to pack snow into a ball."

Maybe the high altitude did something to me. Suddenly I became almost giddy with happiness. I felt free and irresponsible. "It was nice of Harry to stay with Grandma and let us go off like this."

"Nice, nothing!" said Steve. "It's only fair!"

"Well, it's my job to look after Grandma."

"Why should it be?" he demanded. "Why shouldn't the two of you take turns?"

The idea of taking turns was still relatively new. Until recently, I had always assumed that I should be the one to look after Grandma because girls were supposed to be better at looking after old people. Even though Grandma favored Harry, it was simply my obligation to take care of her.

Splat! Something wet and stinging struck the back of my neck. I whirled around and found Steve innocently looking at the horizon.

Furiously, I gathered up a fistful of snow and threw it at him without even taking time to form it into a snowball.

In no time we were thrashing in a blizzard of snow and laughing hard enough to burst.

We had to stop when our hands ached fiercely from the cold. I stuffed my fingers in my mouth to warm them. "I think I'm getting frostbite. How long does it take for your fingers to turn black and fall off?"

In the mountains you can freeze even in August, especially when your jeans and sweatshirt are wet. "We'd better get back," said Steve. His teeth were chattering.

As we came down the steep trail toward the visitors' center, we could see someone running uphill, waving his arms in the air.

"Isn't that Harry?" asked Steve.

"It sure looks like Harry," I said slowly, "except that Harry doesn't run — especially not uphill."

But it *was* Harry, and he was shouting at us, saying something about Grandma. By the time we reached him, Harry was gasping and his face was haggard.

"I can't find Grandma anywhere!" he finally managed to wheeze. "Have you . . . have you seen her?"

Already cold, I felt tiny ice daggers stabbing into my back. "You think she wandered off?"

"She's not in the visitors' center," Harry panted. "I looked all over for her."

"Maybe she's in the ladies' room," said Steve.

"I asked," insisted Harry. He had a wild look, which I had never seen before in my easygoing brother. "I asked every woman who came out of there! I asked everybody in that damn visitors' center!"

I refused to share his panic. Just when Steve and I were enjoying ourselves so much, Grandma had to pull another disappearing act! "Somebody must have seen her," I said. "After all, a little old Chinese woman is someone people would notice."

"I think she's probably in the center, some-where," said Steve.

Harry was taking deep breaths. "Look, I checked all the exhibition rooms. I asked at the reception desk. I looked in the cafe and the souvenir shop." His voice became shrill. "The damnedest thing is that nobody even *saw* her!"

I tried to stay calm. "Maybe you and Harry can check the trails," I said to Steve, "while I check the hotel and the parking lot. I don't think Grandma could have gone far. She can't walk very fast."

I checked the garbage cans behind the res-taurant, but there was no sign of Grandma. Next I asked inside the lodge, a rustic hotel with a restaurant and a store selling Indian ar-tifacts. Nobody had seen an elderly Chinese woman. They were positive.

The ranger station! They might have news. At least they would know what to do in the case of a missing person.

When I told the ranger that my grandmother was not a hiker and could not walk very far, he relaxed. "We send out the helicopters only when people are deep in the mountains. Your grandmother is probably somewhere close by. Have you tried the souvenir shops? Those are the most likely places."

I held on to my temper. "Yes, of course I tried the shops, both at the visitors' center and at the lodge."

The ranger turned grave, however, when I told him that Grandma was diabetic. "That's bad. Okay, I'll get a search party together."

Leaving the ranger's cabin, we came face-to-face with Father and Ellen. They were holding hands, and they were laughing.

"So there you are," Father said when he saw me. "I've never seen such flowers! Whole hills of lupin, Indian paintbrush, Queen Anne's lace, and phlox! We came across a marmot. He rolled over and played dead."

He stopped laughing when he saw my expression. "What's the matter, April?"

"Harry can't find Grandma," I said, and suddenly tears flooded my eyes.

Ellen came over and put her arms around me. "What did Harry say, exactly?"

"He was supposed to watch her!" snapped Father. He looked more angry than alarmed. "She can't have gone far."

"That's what we're hoping," said the ranger. "We'll try all the trails leading from Paradise Park. Meanwhile, I suggest you ask at the souvenir shops again. Maybe one of the customers saw her."

I was still in the souvenir shop when Harry and Steve returned. One look at their faces told me that they had found no trace of Grandma.

An hour later, she was still missing. The ranger and his crew, plus some student volunteer helpers, had all combed the mountainside. None of them could find any evidence that Grandma had been on the trails. They had asked every hiker they met, and no one had seen a sign of her.

"Does she need insulin shots?" asked the ranger. "Maybe I should call in a medic and an ambulance."

"No," said Father. "But she should have food at regular intervals. It's been almost three hours since we had our picnic."

"I was just having a word with the girl at the cafeteria," said Harry. His voice trembled and he looked much younger, somehow. "I swear we didn't chat for more than a couple of minutes. And then — poof! — Grandma disappeared into thin air."

That was the puzzle. After all, wouldn't you think people would notice an elderly, chubby Chinese woman, wearing a Chinese dress, with gray hair gathered in a bun? How could she have left the mountain without *anyone* seeing her?

Ellen reached over and took Father's hand. Earlier they had held hands, but now she clutched him fiercely for a moment and then let go. "I'm sorry, Gilbert."

Our family looked gray-green with fatigue. And guilt. I *knew* I should have stayed behind with Grandma. How could I possibly expect Harry to do a good job of watching her? He had never had any practice!

Guilt. Father was sorry he had gone with Ellen, and Harry was sorry he had talked to the girl in the cafeteria.

Wait a minute! I suddenly remembered Grandma's birthday banquet. She had gone off to join another party because she had become fed up with her own. Could she have joined another party here on Mount Rainier? If so, how did she do it without anybody noticing?

"You said you saw a marmot, Dad," I said to Father. "Don't they change the color of their fur in winter, for protective color?"

For a moment Father just stared at me. "You're thinking of weasels changing to er-mine — or is it the other way around?"

"What are you talking about, April?" demanded Harry. "What does any of this crap have to do with Grandma's disappearance?"

"I think Grandma found protective color," I said.

I'M GOING to the lodge," I said.

"But we went already!" cried Harry. "We asked the shop assistants, the restaurant people, even the customers. We asked everybody!"

"We didn't ask the right question," I said, turning toward the wooden building with the steeply pitched roof.

Steve caught up with me. He understood. "Ermine on snow, right?"

"What are you guys talking about?" panted Harry, running after us.

"If you're an old Chinese woman trying to hide yourself," I said, "what's the best way to do it?"

"By putting yourself in the middle of a

bunch of other old Chinese women," Steve told Harry.

Harry stopped dead. There were angry, white patches around his mouth. "I don't believe it! You're making it sound like Grandma is deliberately hiding just to scare us!"

I didn't say anything and just rushed on. He caught up with me and grabbed my arm. "Did you see a bunch of old Chinese women on Mount Rainier?" he demanded. "I didn't!"

We came up to the front desk of the lodge. "Is there a group of Asian tourists staying here?" I asked the receptionist.

The receptionist shook his head. "I don't think so, but I'll check." He consulted the registration book and again shook his head. "Sorry. There's no group party staying tonight."

I sagged with disappointment. I had been so sure!

Father and Ellen came in. "No luck?" asked Father.

The voice of the receptionist said, "But we do have reservations made for a Japanese tour group planning to stay for dinner."

Bingo! Steve and I looked at each other, and we both nodded. I turned back to the desk. "Where are the tourists now? When are they coming back?"

"The dinner reservation is for six," replied the receptionist, "but I don't know where they are now. Just a minute."

He turned and called to a girl walking out of the dining room. "Hey, Susie, you were talking to some of those Japanese tourists a while ago. Did they say where they were going?"

Susie considered. "Yeah, one of the women said their tour guide was taking them to the Reflection Lakes area. Great photo opportunities there."

The Reflection Lakes weren't far from Paradise Park. Even allowing for the most tireless photographer, the tour group should be back before long.

"You think Grandma is with those tourists?" asked Father.

I nodded. "I can't think of any other way she could have disappeared so completely from Paradise Park."

"What does she get out of it?" demanded Ellen furiously. "She can't speak a word of Japanese!"

"We can ask her," I said, staring out the window of the lodge. Relief and exasperation swept over me. "Because here she comes."

A young Japanese woman entered the lodge first, carrying a pointed yellow flag on a stick.

Following docilely behind her was a file of elderly Japanese tourists, the majority of them women. Grandma entered the lodge walking between two of the women. She was about as inconspicuous as a white-coated ermine on snow.

Grandma waved good-bye to her two Japanese companions. *"Sayonara,"* she said.

The two women giggled. *"Zaijian,"* they said, with a tolerably good Chinese accent. They bowed before going away with the rest of their group.

I walked up slowly to Grandma and with an effort managed to keep my voice casual. "Did you have a good time, Grandma? The receptionist said your group would be back by now."

Grandma turned to me. "So you knew where I was?" To my surprise, I saw a look of respect in her eyes.

"Steve and I guessed that you went off with this group. But what on earth made you do it?"

Father couldn't act as well as I could. He rushed up to Grandma and crushed her in a hug. "You had us all worried sick!"

"The rest of you were all away and enjoying yourselves," said Grandma. "I had nothing to do."

She was trying to sound like an old woman abandoned by her family. I *knew* she was.

"So when one of the Japanese women was asking the salesgirl about a Navajo rug," continued Grandma, "I went over to give her some advice."

"But, Mother, you don't know anything about Navajo rugs!" said Father.

"What does that have to do with it?" retorted Grandma. "That Japanese tourist would go home happy, thinking she got a good bargain. Whereas if I hadn't advised her, she would always wonder if she had bought the right thing."

Father stared at Grandma. "But how did you communicate? You don't speak any Japanese!"

"We managed to share a certain amount of English," Grandma said modestly. "We also communicated a little by writing. The Chinese characters mean the same in Japanese."

"Yes, but didn't you realize how worried we'd be when we came back to find you gone?" cried Harry. He had never used that harsh tone of voice with her before.

"When you went away, I was lonely," replied Grandma with a forlorn little smile. "The Japanese tourists offered me company."

"I was gone only for a minute!" yelled Harry. I felt an unholy joy at seeing Harry suffer from one of Grandma's shenanigans for a change.

"I only wanted to have some fun, too," murmured Grandma.

Ellen exploded. "This is ridiculous!"

Father frowned. "You'll have to explain yourself, Ellen," he said coldly.

"Don't you see what she's doing to you?" cried Ellen. "After scaring us out of our wits, she's making us feel that it's all *our* fault!"

"All I can see is that my mother is back at last," Father said. "I should think you'd be relieved to see her safe and sound."

Ellen sputtered. "Safe and sound? But there was never any question of her safety!"

Although I knew Ellen was right, I could see she was going to lose this battle. She was fighting with the wrong weapon: She was using yang instead of yin, a head-on confrontation instead of subtlety.

"When a frail old woman is missing on top of a snow-covered mountain," said Father, "any decent person would worry about her safety!"

"She was missing because she chose to leave!" said Ellen. Her voice was becoming shrill. "When are you going to open your eyes

139

and see what your mother is doing to you? To all of you?"

I stole a glance at Steve. Was he embarrassed by this public quarrel? He was looking at Ellen, and he seemed to realize she was losing.

When Father did not reply, Ellen spun on her heel. "I'm going home."

"But Ellen, you can't . . . ," began Father.

Without looking back Ellen rushed out of the lodge and into the parking lot. Father started to follow her.

"I think I'd like something to eat," Grandma said in a shaking voice.

Alarm bells went off in my head. "Oh, my gosh, Grandma! Your blood sugar level!"

Father turned and looked reproachfully at Harry. "You should have bought Grandma something to eat."

Harry seemed close to tears. "I know. Everything's my fault!"

"You haven't eaten anything in all this time, Grandma?" I asked.

"One of those Japanese women gave me some rice crackers," she said with a long-suffering sigh. "But it wasn't much."

We crowded into the snack bar and ordered hot dogs. Restored by food, Grandma began to chatter. She told us that the Japanese tourists had been impressed by her knowledge of Mount Rainier, and almost everyone in the party had posed for a picture with her.

"Where's Harry?" Steve suddenly asked.

I looked around and realized that Harry had not joined us in the snack bar.

At that moment, Harry came in. "Hey, I'd like a hot dog, too."

"Where have you been?" I asked. "We've had enough disappearances today."

"I wanted to say good-bye to Ellen," Harry said. "I guess she's already gone. Her car isn't there anymore."

Father looked at Harry in surprise and then went back to staring down miserably at his hot dog. I was surprised, too. So Ellen's words must have got through to Harry. Even he now realized that Grandma had spoiled our outing deliberately.

Grandma's victory wasn't complete, though. She hadn't expected Harry to go over to the enemy.

OUR PHONE was in the hallway, and several times since the picnic I overheard Father trying to call Ellen. His sentences were abruptly broken off, and from the way he winced, I knew

141

that Ellen had hung up on him. Grandma didn't even try to hide her satisfaction after each of his unsuccessful calls.

"Is Ellen still mad at your Dad?" asked Steve.

It was fall, and school had started. Steve and I were now seniors at Garfield High, and we had come back from watching our school win the first football game of the season. I had invited Steve over for supper. He was now openly coming to the house.

At Steve's question, I looked around before replying. Grandma was apparently still upstairs resting.

"I'm not sure how things are between Ellen and Dad," I said. "He's tried calling her several times, but she's hung up on him."

Rattling sounds of pots and pans came from the kitchen. "Who's out there doing the cooking?" asked Steve.

"That's Mrs. Li," I said, lowering my voice. "I told you about her. You know, the young widow from China." I pointed to the little boy sitting in front of the television set. "That's her son."

The boy might not understand English, but he turned on hearing the name Li. His eyes widened at the sight of Steve, and he rose from his chair.

"Hi," said Steve, smiling at the boy.

After a moment, the boy returned the smile. He turned back avidly to the TV set, which was showing a commercial with dozens of cars crashing noisily into each other.

"I don't know how much English he understands," I said, "but he sure loves to watch commercials. He likes them better than the programs themselves. The commercials on Chinese TV must be pretty boring."

"I guess he'll be back to watching Chinese TV pretty soon," said Steve. "I feel kind of sorry for the kid."

"I feel sorry for his mother, too," I said. "She'll have to go back when her visa expires . . . unless . . . ."

"Unless what?"

"Unless she marries an American citizen. Then she and her son will be able to stay."

After a pause, Steve asked, "You think your grandmother is still working on that?"

"Maybe it's all in my imagination," I said slowly. "But now that Ellen seems to be breaking up with Dad, Grandma is *really* pushing Mrs. Li at him. This is already the third time she's invited her over. It's getting pretty embarrassing. . . ."

I stopped as I heard slow steps on the stairs. Grandma had got up from her nap.

When she saw Steve, she nodded. It wasn't exactly a warm welcome — more like grudging acceptance. At least it was an improvement over calling him a foreign devil and ignoring him.

"I'll see how things are going in the kitchen," Grandma said. "Where is your father?"

I realized that Father was usually home by now. "Dad didn't say anything about coming home late."

A few minutes later, the front door opened, but it was Harry. His nose twitched at the delicious smells coming out of the kitchen. When he caught sight of the little boy, however, his eyebrows rose. "We're having the Lis over again?"

"Grandma invited them," I said. "They're nice people and everything, but . . ."

"Yeah, I know what you mean," said Harry. "Grandma is thinking of making them a permanent fixture here, isn't she? What about Ellen?"

Ever since the Mount Rainier picnic, Harry had been rather cool toward Grandma, especially in the matter of Ellen.

Grandma emerged from the kitchen. If she heard Harry's question, she showed no signs of it. "The food is almost ready," she announced.

"I'll go set the table," I said.

"I'll help you," said Steve, getting up. He sank back on seeing the outrage on Grandma's face.

"In this household, boys don't do any of the housework," I told him out of the corner of my mouth.

I was counting out the chopsticks when the phone rang. "Shall I get it, or don't boys answer the phone, either?" asked Steve.

Harry picked up the phone. After listening for a minute, he nodded and said, "Good work, Dad!"

When he came back to the dining room, he was grinning. "That was Dad. He's not coming home for dinner. He managed to persuade Ellen to have dinner with him at that new seafood place on the waterfront."

Grandma, who had been talking to the little boy, turned around slowly. Her face was like a block of ice.

I was delighted for Father, but I knew we'd have an uncomfortable dinner ahead of us. It turned out to be even more excruciating than I expected. I felt so sorry for Mrs. Li, who had slaved over the meal, that the food stuck in my throat.

Steve sensed our discomfort and didn't seem to be enjoying himself, either. Grandma sat imperiously at the head of the table, hardly touching her food. Mrs. Li and her son ate with their heads bent over their rice bowls. Of all the people at the table, only Harry was in a good mood. He ate lavishly, praising Mrs. Li's cooking at one moment and at the next moment chuckling over Father's success with Ellen. I wanted to empty the soup tureen over him.

At last the meal ended. Mrs. Li rose from the table and said that she had to be going.

"We'll drive you home, Mrs. Li," I said.

At the front door, Mrs. Li turned to Grandma, and there were tears in her eyes. "Thank you for having us."

There was no answering emotion on Grandma's face. But when she looked down at the little boy, she softened. "Good-bye, Harry," she said, her voice becoming slightly husky. She patted him on the head, and her touch was very gentle. A long, long time ago, I thought, she had patted me the same way.

The drive to Mrs. Li's place was short, and hardly a word was said. Steve was driving, and Mrs. Li sat in front with him. She shrank from him as much as she could in the limited space, as if the foreign devil might turn and bite her in the neck.

I sat in the backseat with the little boy and tried hard to think of something to say to him. Finally I asked him if he enjoyed the TV commercials. Since I couldn't think of the Chinese word for *commercials*, what I actually said was, "Did you enjoy the propaganda?"

He just blinked and stared at me.

When we arrived, Mrs. Li and her son got out of the car. "I don't think we'll see you again," she said softly. "We're going home next Monday. Please tell your grandmother that we appreciate her kindness to us." Her voice trembled a little at the end.

It was heartbreaking, the sight of Mrs. Li and her son waving at us as we drove off. "God, I feel dreadful," I said.

"Because they have to go back to China?" asked Steve. "You said they had visitors' visas, so they knew they couldn't stay."

"Grandma led them on. She made Mrs. Li think Dad might get interested in her. And now she sees how hopeless it all is."

"Yeah," said Steve. "If she had hopes there, she must be feeling awfully disappointed. Your grandmother is probably disappointed, too."

"It serves her right," I muttered. I couldn't feel any sympathy for Grandma. What she had done to Mrs. Li was cruel. Even if she had meant well, she shouldn't have played around with other people's hopes and feelings like that.

I was determined not to let her do the same to me.

ELEVEN

*I*T WAS TWO WEEKS before the SAT. A group of kids in my class planned to go over some old exams together to prepare for the actual SAT.

I knew that Father was taking Ellen to a play, so I approached Harry. "Are you busy tonight?"

"What do you mean?" he asked cautiously.

"Can you stay home with Grandma? Dad is going out with Ellen, and I want to practice taking old SAT exams with some friends."

Harry shrugged. "You don't really have to practice, April. You'll do just fine."

I tried to keep my temper. "Does that mean

you can't stay home? Or does it mean you won't?"

"Of course I'd like to help you out," Harry said, and he sounded completely sincere. "But I've got this really important problem set that's due pretty soon."

I could feel the steam building up inside of me. "Look, Harry. I've already given up orchestra and several outings with the Rock Hounds because of looking after Grandma. I admit that your schoolwork is more important than my after-school activities. But the SAT is different. My whole future could depend on how well I do on the test."

"Come on, April, cut the sob story. You'll need violins next."

I held onto my temper, but it took everything I had. "What about *your* sob stories? All those hard problem sets and why you have to stay out so late to work on them!"

"I'm willing to bet real money that you'll do just fine on the SAT, April."

Since birth I had been resigned to the fact that a daughter was less important than a son. It had only been recently, with Steve's help and Ellen's, that I'd begun to question this. But what could I do? Even if I was changing, Harry wasn't.

Then I got my great idea. Maybe Steve could come over to my house and we could study the old exams together! Our family accepted him now. He had spent a whole day with us on the trip to Mount Rainier. Since then he had eaten supper at our house and had proved that he could manipulate chopsticks as well as any of us.

That night he manipulated his chopsticks on the stir-fried prawns and peas. It's not easy to pick up a pea with your chopsticks, even if you're an old hand. Steve did so well that Harry gave a cheer, and even Grandma smiled.

Her smile disappeared when Father announced that he was going out. He radiated so much happiness that he might as well have been wearing a neon sign on his chest spelling *Ellen*. I gave him a thumbs-up sign as he was going out the door, and in reply he twirled his umbrella with a flourish.

Next Harry announced that he was going to the university library. That left me and Steve. He knew better than to offer to help me with the dishes, but when I was through, he brought over a pile of old exams that he had checked out of the library and spread them out on the dining table.

Grandma's eyebrows rose. "What are you two planning to do?"

"We're studying together," I explained. "We're going to coach each other on these exams, to prepare ourselves for the real one."

"You've never studied with anyone before," she said, frowning. "Harry doesn't need a friend to come over to help him study."

That's because Harry can go out whenever he wants to study with his friends, I thought, while *I* have to stay home and look after you. I wanted very much to say it aloud but managed to restrain myself.

"Besides, you always study at your desk, not down here on the dining table," added Grandma.

"If we're in your way, Grandma, we'll go upstairs to my room, then."

Grandma's eyes bulged with horror. "Certainly not! What are you thinking of?"

"Well, then," I said sweetly, "if you don't mind, we'll get down to work."

For half an hour we worked very hard, and I began to get the feeling that I might do okay, after all. We started with the geometry part of the math section, which was what I was best at. Steve fed me the questions and gave me exactly four minutes for each one. I didn't know how long I'd have on the real test, but we had decided to put more pressure on ourselves with a time limit.

In the middle of reading out one of the questions, Steve's voice suddenly began to shake. I raised my head from my piece of scratch paper and saw that he was looking at Grandma and trying very hard not to laugh.

She was sitting in the living room with a piece of knitting in her hands. She had placed her armchair in such a way that she had a full view of us both, and her eyes drilled into us like twin laser beams.

"I hope we're not keeping your grandma from her knitting," Steve whispered to me.

"Don't worry about it," I whispered back. "She hates to knit, anyway."

Steve looked surprised. "No kidding! But she makes such a perfect picture, knitting that gray sweater — almost like an ad for lamb's wool, or something."

I giggled. "Listen, she started that sweater for Harry when he was a boy, and it wasn't gray in the beginning; it started out as baby-blue."

We went back to the tests, and it was my turn to feed questions to Steve. He did pretty well at first. We were on trig problems, and he had a good head for figures. But soon his answers got slower and slower. "I can't concentrate," he confessed, "not with your grandma's eyes drilling holes in me."

"Why don't we take a break," I suggested. "I know what—let's bring the tests to the kitchen and work there."

We each had some Pepsi and a couple of almond cookies, and then buckled down to work again. A few minutes later, Grandma came into the kitchen and put the kettle on. "I need a cup of tea," she said blandly. "I'm getting thirsty. Do you and your friend want some, April?"

I shook my head. We tried to get back to the tests, but it was hard going, with Grandma opening and shutting cupboards in the kitchen and rummaging around. "Where did that can of bamboo shoots go?" she muttered.

Steve sighed and got up. "Maybe we'd better go back to the dining table."

We sat down in the dining room again, and less than five minutes later, Grandma returned to her armchair and her knitting and her penetrating stare.

Why was she doing this? Was she afraid that we'd get up to no good the minute she blinked? Suddenly another thought occurred to me: Was Grandma deliberately distracting me because she didn't want me to do well on the SAT? But why? After all, Chinese families want their kids to do well in their studies — even girls.

"Grandma will get sleepy eventually," I told Steve, "and then she'll have to go to bed."

At the mention of sleepiness, Steve smothered a yawn. "I might have to pack it in before your grandma does. If you ask me, she seems good for another eight hours."

Maybe Grandma thought that if I did well on the SAT, I would get accepted by the college of my choice, which was in Colorado. For a moment, I was touched by the thought that she might miss me if I went away. Or would she only miss my ability to run her errands?

Whatever the reason, I was determined not to let her spoil the study session. "We can wear her out," I said to Steve.

We set up a routine: we'd work at the dining table for twenty minutes, then go to the kitchen for a bite and work there for twenty minutes, and then go back to the dining table and start the whole thing all over again.

By ten o'clock, we had made some progress. I was feeling a bit tired myself, while Grandma was beginning to stumble as she chased after us. I felt a twinge of guilt, but I didn't give up. In the end, we won because we were young and fit, and Grandma was old and diabetic.

As we sat down at the dining table again — was it the fourth or the fifth round? — and talked in a low voice, I heard a faint snore from the living room. Grandma's head fell forward, and her knitting dropped to the ground.

In sleep, Grandma's face looked as smooth as a girl's. My heart suddenly filled with pity and exasperation — and love. Fetching a lap blanket from the closet, I gently tucked it around her.

"She seems so innocent, doesn't she?" said Steve. "I feel like a real louse, wearing her out like that."

I picked up the piece of knitting, the old unfinished sweater that she had been using as a prop all these years. "Let's get back to work."

I found most of the math questions pretty easy, but I did less well on the verbal parts, especially in the questions where I had to find synonyms. With the help of the almond cookies, Steve went through the verbal questions like a breeze.

We finished the last of the tests by eleven.

Steve looked at his watch. "Oh, my God, look at the time! I've got to run!"

As I closed the front door after Steve's warm good-night kiss, I felt gloriously happy.

Father got back soon after Steve left. "How was the play?" I asked him.

"It was all right," he said, smiling a little. I had the impression that he hadn't noticed the play much.

He looked startled when he caught sight of Grandma in the living room. "Why is Grandma sleeping here, instead of in her own room?"

I laughed. "She was doing her darnedest to act as chaperon."

Grandma stirred and opened her eyes. Then she looked around wildly. "Where is the foreign devil?"

"Steve?" I couldn't keep a note of triumph from my voice. "We finished going through all the sample tests, so he left."

Without a word, Grandma struggled to her feet. Father rushed over to help her, but she shook him off irritably. She was in a bad mood as she climbed up the stairs to her room.

"What's the matter with Grandma?" asked Father.

"She's just mad because she couldn't stay

awake to watch us," I said airily. I was feeling pretty pleased with myself.

I TOOK THE SAT in November. When the results came, I learned that my scores were pretty good, probably high enough to get me accepted at the Colorado School of Mines.

"But how could I go away to college?" I asked Steve, as we sat over our root beer floats in the Burger King. "Who would look after Grandma?"

Steve pulled at his straw with a loud gurgle. "You know, something's been puzzling me for a long time. Why do you feel that it's *your* job to look after your grandma? Why can't your dad do it for a change? Or Harry?"

His question caught me by surprise, and then I was surprised at my own surprise. Of course, he must be wondering why *I* felt responsible for Grandma. Father was actually the one who was closest to her, and by rights she should really be his responsibility. Harry, her adored grandson, her treasure, should shoulder his part of the burden, too. I was only a girl, the person least important to Grandma. So why was I the one who was worrying the most about her?

I looked up at Steve. "Okay, so tell me this:

if I went away to college and left Grandma alone at home, what do you think would happen?"

"Well . . ." Steve took another pull at his root beer float, but all he got was bubbles. "Well, your dad would have to come up with something. It's his job, after all."

"What sort of thing did you have in mind?"

Steve blinked. "Well, maybe something like a baby-sitter . . . you know . . . someone who comes in and keeps your grandma company when your dad and Harry go out in the evenings."

I wanted to laugh. "Can you picture Grandma putting up with a teenage baby-sitter? Remember I told you about the nurse at the doctor's office? Grandma made her look ridiculous! She's like Dennis the Menace. She'd never get the same baby-sitter twice."

Steve shook his head. "I still don't get it. I admit that it won't be easy to get someone to look after your grandma, but I still say it's your *dad's* problem."

He just didn't understand. In a Chinese family, women were the care givers. If Mother had been alive, she would be the one who was responsible for Grandma's care. Now it was my problem.

We were so far apart, Steve and I. I had

told Grandma that I was an American, that I was proud to salute the flag. Now I realized that I was looking at Steve across a gulf. I twisted my plastic drinking straw around my finger, until it cut off the circulation and turned the finger purple. "What if I went away to college and then heard that Grandma got into a diabetic coma because nobody was around? Or that Ellen broke up with Dad because she didn't want to be saddled with Grandma? How could I live with myself afterward?"

"It's not your fault every time something bad happens in the world," protested Steve.

"I'm not saying I'm responsible for the whole world!" I cried. "Chinese family ties are very strong, and I do feel responsible for what happens to my own family."

Steve was silent for a long time. "I guess I do understand — sort of," he said finally. "Different people have different customs, as I keep telling myself."

He said he understood, but I could see that he really didn't. Yet he was doing his best to meet me halfway. I swallowed hard and blinked back my tears.

"You'll think of a way out, April," he said gently. "You're no dummy. Hey, remember how you got around your Grandma that night

160

we studied for the SAT?" He suddenly smiled. "Actually, you're kind of alike, you and your grandmother."

I was shocked. "Alike? Grandma is ruthless and manipulative! Is that how you see me?"

He shook his head. "You're alike because you're both fighters."

I was not flattered. "You really think I'm ready to use people like poor Mrs. Li in order to get my way?"

"Your grandma uses the weapons available to her. Maybe she doesn't have any choice."

Grandma used the weapon of yin and worked deviously in the dark because her society forced her to. I belonged to a different society, so maybe I could work out in the open. But how?

OTHER CHINESE FAMILIES had problems with aging grandmothers, too. How did they deal with the problems?

Our friends, the Liangs, gave us an idea of what the future might bring. Mrs. Liang's daughter, Phyllis, had had to place her mother in the Green Haven Nursing Home, which had been set up with the help of the Seattle Chinese community and catered mainly to elderly Chinese.

"I'm going over to the Green Haven Nursing Home to bring Mrs. Liang some Chinese novels," Father told me. "What do you think of the idea of taking Grandma?"

He looked undecided, and I didn't blame

him. "It might depress Grandma to see her old friend looking so frail and helpless," I said.

"This Chinese nursing home is different from a huge, impersonal hospital," said Father. "The fact is, I'm curious to see if Grandma would like the place, in case . . . in case . . . well, in case her diabetes gets so bad she needs around-the-clock care."

Or in case she's getting too senile to run around loose, I thought. Anyway, this was our chance to see how Grandma reacted to the place. The atmosphere of the Chinese nursing home might be cheerful and friendly. We wouldn't lose anything by taking a look.

"I'd like to go with you," I said. "I'm curious about the place myself."

Grandma did not seem enthusiastic about visiting her friend. "Marsha Liang has always been a wishy-washy kind of person," she muttered. "Trust her to wind up in a place like that."

I was shocked. "Grandma! Mrs. Liang has been your best friend for almost fifty years! How can you say that?"

"She was a good bridge partner," admitted Grandma. "But she doesn't play anymore. She can't keep her mind on her cards."

Why is it that old people are a lot less sentimental than young people, I wondered. They probably can't afford to be. Since they keep losing their friends as the years pass, they have to harden themselves.

Grandma eventually consented to go to the Green Haven Nursing Home. "Just this once," she said grudgingly. "Perhaps I can talk Marsha into leaving the place and going back home."

Father and I looked at each other in alarm. Maybe we shouldn't have asked Grandma to go, after all. But she was already standing at the door, ready to leave. Having worked so hard at persuading her, how could we tell her not to go?

The Green Haven Nursing Home was on a hill south of Chinatown. From the front there was a panoramic view of Puget Sound and the Olympic Mountains. The grounds looked well-groomed and spacious. I saw some residents being pushed around the garden in wheelchairs, and their voices were cheerful. On the south side of the building we saw a vegetable garden, and a couple of elderly men were bent over the plants, engrossed in caring for them.

At the front desk, we pinned on buttons identifying ourselves as visitors and then took the elevator to the third floor, where Mrs. Liang was.

As the elevator door opened on the third

floor, we stepped out and found ourselves facing a semicircle of elderly Chinese. It looked like a coffee klatch, except that they were all in wheelchairs. When the residents saw us, their faces fell and they turned back to one another. I wanted to apologize for not being a visitor for one of the expectant circle.

None of the people at the elevator was Mrs. Liang. The nurse at the desk told us that she was resting in her room. We found Mrs. Liang in bed. When she saw us, she raised her head and greeted us wanly. "Phyllis called and told me you were coming. Sorry I'm lying down like this. They just gave me a bath, and my hip is so painful that I can't sit up."

"You're looking well, Auntie Liang," said Father, obviously lying. He handed over a pile of Chinese paperback novels.

Grandma's lips were turned down. Perhaps she didn't enjoy picturing herself in Mrs. Liang's place.

"What do people here do all day?" she asked. "We saw them sitting around in front of the elevator. Is that how they spend their time?"

Mrs. Liang tried to raise her shoulders, then grimaced and lay back. "They like to sit there watching the elevator doors open, in case relatives or friends arrive."

I was shocked. "Then there's nothing else to do here at all?"

"There are all sorts of activities," said Mrs. Liang. "They show Chinese movies here every afternoon."

"Oh, really?" Father exclaimed brightly. "I love Chinese movies, but I don't often get a chance to see them."

"They're mostly kung fu movies from Hong Kong," Mrs. Liang said glumly. "I can't stand them. All that kicking and fighting."

"I saw people playing mah-jongg in the lounge," said Grandma.

"Oh, there are some pretty lively people here," Mrs. Liang said. Was she being sarcastic?

"How's the food?" asked Father. "Do they serve Chinese food or Western food?"

For the first time, Mrs. Liang broke into a genuine smile. "Chinese food. And it's pretty good, too, better than what I've been getting at home." She added hurriedly, "I'm not complaining about Phyllis's cooking, but she's too busy to spend much time on food."

"If there's anything you need or want, we'd be glad to get it for you," offered Father. "The Chinese grocery is just down the street."

"Thank you, but Phyllis brings me everything I need," Mrs. Liang said. "In fact, here she is!"

Phyllis Liang looked older than her true age, which was the same as Father's. When she saw us, she smiled with real pleasure and immediately looked years younger. "Auntie Chen!" she cried. "You're much too kind, to come visiting! But I can see that Mother is delighted to see you!"

The two old friends of fifty years regarded each other with less than total delight. I wondered if Mrs. Liang was a little jealous of Grandma's relative good health.

"Maybe I'll look in on one of the mah-jongg games," said Grandma, getting up and going to the door.

"Mother," gasped Father, "we just got here! Aren't you going to visit longer with your friend?"

"Let her go," said Mrs. Liang, sighing. "Mei-yun has always been on the move."

After Grandma left, there was an embarrassed silence. Then Father and Phyllis Liang began to chat about the Saturday Chinese classes they used to attend together. Mrs. Liang remembered helping Grandma run the annual bazaar, which made money for the school. Her voice gradually grew weaker, and we could tell that she was tired.

We said our farewells and got ready to go. In the lounge we found Grandma. Of course, she had inserted herself as the fourth player in a game of mah-jongg.

I was glad. After so many old acquaintances had died, Grandma seldom found enough people to make a foursome for mah-jongg or bridge. It was nice to see her happily wrapped up in the game.

Father must have felt the same. "Let's not interrupt the game. I want to have a talk with the director of the Green Haven."

The director was a slender, middle-aged Chinese-American who had grown up speaking Cantonese. But he also spoke Mandarin. "About forty percent of our patients here are Mandarin speakers," he said, "and the percentage is increasing because more of the recent immigrants are from the north. Most of our staff here speak both dialects."

"That should be good for my mother, then," said Father.

"You are contemplating sending your mother here?" asked the director.

Father looked uncomfortable. "It's a possibility. My mother has diabetes, and she is also beginning to behave a little strangely."

There was a faint sound in the corridor. I looked around and saw Grandma outside the door. How long had she been standing there? How much had she overheard?

Grandma was carrying several small packages in her hands. "What are those, Mother?" asked Father.

"My winnings," she replied. She displayed the packages, which turned out to be a couple of "hundred-year-old" eggs still in their coating of lime, a package of pickled turnip, and a hair clip with most of the bronze coating chipped off. "The others didn't have money on them, you see," she explained.

"You — you mean you played for . . .," stammered Father.

"There's no point in playing mah-jongg unless you play for stakes," Grandma said coolly. She frowned. "It wasn't much fun playing with them. They weren't very good."

With the director's sardonic gaze on us, Father and I hurried Grandma out of the office. As we walked down the corridor, we heard sounds of weeping.

"My hair clip," cried a pathetic voice. "What am I going to do with my hair?"

We couldn't get out of the nursing home fast enough. After this, the Green Haven, with its long waiting list, would be unlikely to rush to admit Grandma in the near future. Perhaps that had been her intention all along?

THE HUNDRED-YEAR-OLD eggs were cut up and served for dinner that night. "Hey, we haven't had these for a long time," said Harry.

"We're eating Grandma's winnings," I said. I told him about the visit to the Green Haven Nursing Home and the mah-jongg game.

Harry looked horrified. "You mean we're taking food from the mouth of some poor old lady?"

I had never seen Grandma look defensive before. Now she had the grace to blush. "She won't starve! From what I hear, they get pretty good food there."

"Yes, but these eggs were probably some special treat brought by her relatives!" said Harry indignantly.

Grandma blinked at Harry's remark and tried to look nonchalant, but I thought that she was hurt.

After dinner, Father came into the kitchen while I was packing the dishes into the dishwasher and scrubbing the saucepans. He picked up a pot and wiped it as we began to chat.

We hadn't done much of it lately because he had been out a lot with Ellen. At first I was a bit jealous. But I did have Steve.

Soon Father got on the subject that was uppermost on his mind. "Ellen's been very patient," he said. "But I don't know how long she's going to wait."

"I know how you feel," I said. "But she really loves you, Dad. She will wait."

He moodily picked up another pot. "She's young and attractive. I'm sure there are lots of men after her."

I smiled at him. "You're young and attractive, too."

He didn't smile back. "She's been seeing that ex-husband of hers. I saw them together in front of the Henry Gallery the other day."

"That doesn't mean they plan to get together again. They're in the same department at the university, and they could be just talking business."

"What attracted Ellen to him in the first place, I wonder," said Father. "For that matter, why did you pick yourself a Caucasian boyfriend, too? There are lots of Chinese boys around—Harry's friends, for instance."

I had known that sooner or later Father would ask me this question. Grandma already had, and my answer was ready. "Harry's friends, like Harry himself, are used to being the family treasure. They think girls exist solely for the purpose of serving them. Steve treats me like an equal. Maybe it was the same with Ellen."

Father put the pot down with a clatter. "Is that how you see all Chinese men?"

I felt a sudden rush of tenderness for him. "Not you, Dad. You're different. Ellen obviously thinks so, too."

But Father still look troubled. "Does that mean you'll marry a white boy someday? Steve, for instance?"

"For heaven's sake, Dad! I'm years away from getting married! Besides, not all Chinese boys are like Harry. I might find somebody nice — like you." I knew I had avoided answering his question, but when Father picked up a pot lid and began to wipe it, I could tell that he was pleased.

We began to talk about school, and it was like old times again. Maybe I was close to Father because we were both underdogs. Father had had to take second place to Uncle Walter in Grandma's favor, and I took second place to Harry.

"How is orchestra?" asked Father.

At the mention of orchestra, I felt a spurt of bitterness. "I dropped out," I said in a low voice.

Father was shocked. "Why? You've always loved it!"

I sighed. "I had to cut too many rehearsals. Somebody had to stay home and look after Grandma—make her a snack between meals, see that she doesn't go wandering off at night . . ."

"Doesn't Harry stay with her occasionally?"

"He always had some reason why he couldn't—a problem set that's due or some lab work to finish up."

I wondered if Father would say that my orchestra rehearsals were just as important as Harry's studies. He didn't. The idea was simply too revolutionary for him.

"I'm sorry, April," he said finally. "I've been thinking so much about my own problems that I didn't realize how much you've had to do for Grandma. I'll try to think of some solution."

Like what? A baby-sitter? A nursing home? I didn't say it aloud. What was the use?

173

We discussed my application to the Colorado School of Mines. "With your SAT scores, you should be able to get into the school," Father said. "By the way, haven't you heard from them yet? It's late."

Actually, most of my friends had already heard from the places they had applied to. I had tried not to worry about it, but now Father's words began to alarm me. "You think if I got in, I should have heard by now?"

"Why don't you check it out? Mail can get lost."

As it turned out, the letter had not been lost.

THIRTEEN

T HE NEXT DAY I asked my counselor at school, and he was surprised that I hadn't heard. "You should have been accepted." Then he added hurriedly, "Of course I can't guarantee that you got in. But you should call up their admissions office."

I hesitated. "I don't want to seem pushy. Maybe they haven't made up their minds yet."

"It's already April," the counselor said. "The letters should have gone out by now."

Trembling with nervousness, I called up the admissions office at the Colorado School of Mines as soon as I got home. When I hung up, I was trembling even more. Now it was from anger.

I should have known. I should have remembered that other important mail had mysteriously disappeared.

I found Grandma in the living room. "Grandma, did you see an official letter that was addressed to me?"

Her face showed no expression. "What letter?"

I tried to keep my temper. "A letter of acceptance from the Colorado School of Mines."

Harry, who was flipping through a magazine, sat up. "No kidding? You got in, April? Congratulations!"

"They told me they sent me a letter of acceptance weeks ago, but I never saw it." I found myself breathing hard. "Did you throw away the letter, Grandma? Don't lie to me. It's beneath you."

"Then I won't lie," Grandma said calmly. "Yes, I threw it away."

"Hey, that's a pretty low thing to do!" said Harry. "I'm surprised at you, Grandma!"

"You keep out of this!" Grandma snapped at him.

At any other time, I would have been delighted to hear her snapping at him, but now I was too angry. "Why, Grandma?" I demanded. "Why did you throw away my letter?"

"A school of mines!" said Grandma contemptuously. "What kind of place is that for a girl? I don't want you mingling with miners."

"The decision is for *me* to make!" I said.

"Furthermore, sending you out there would be expensive," added Grandma. "We'd have to pay for your room and board, besides the tuition."

"Dad makes the decision about whether or not he wants to pay for my fees!" Indignation rose in me like a hot tide.

"In a proper Chinese family, the mother makes all the decisions about money," Grandma said crisply.

Suddenly my anger poured out, breaking through the years of upbringing by my mother and grandmother. "There's been a revolution in China! So you don't even know what a proper Chinese family is!"

"Revolutions don't change the true Chinese character," declared Grandma.

"We're not living in China!" I shouted. "We're living in America, in case you haven't noticed!"

"You'll never be a real American, no matter how long you live here," said Grandma. "You're Chinese. You look Chinese. You can't change your skin, your hair, your eyes."

Grandma's words were all the more hurtful because I had said them to myself before. I refused to accept them. "Are you blind? Look around you! Americans come in all shapes!"

"Calm down, calm down, April!" said Harry.

"Oh, shut up, Harry!" I said furiously.

"I did it for your own good, April," said Grandma. She looked shaken.

I wasn't fooled by her look of helpless frailty this time. "I won't let you interfere with my life ever again!"

Grandma shrank back. No one had shouted at her like that for years, perhaps not since Grandpa had died — perhaps never.

AT DINNER that night, I told Father about my acceptance. He smiled. "That's wonderful, April. I'm very proud of you."

"I almost didn't find out about it because Grandma threw away my letter of acceptance," I said grimly.

Father looked quickly at Grandma. He opened his mouth, and I had a wild hope that he might reproach Grandma. Then he closed it again. He could not escape his upbringing: He was still too much the dutiful Chinese son to reproach his mother. The fact that I had done so proved how much *I* had changed in recent months.

I wondered what he would have said if he had heard me shouting at Grandma earlier.

Grandma rose abruptly from the table and walked out of the dining room. I didn't care.

But I should have realized that Grandma would try to have the last word.

After dinner, when I had finished the dishes and walked into the living room, only Father and Harry were sitting there.

"Where's Grandma?" I asked.

Father looked up from the newspapers. "I thought she was in the kitchen talking to you."

"No, she hasn't been in the kitchen." I remembered the abrupt way Grandma had got up from the dining table, and I began to feel uneasy.

"Maybe she went up to her room," suggested Harry. He looked nervously at me.

We couldn't find Grandma anywhere in the house.

"She's just doing this to frighten us," I said to Father. "Remember when she got us into a panic on Mount Rainier?"

Father blinked. "But why is she doing something like that now? On Mount Rainier, she was angry because I went in Ellen's car, I thought."

Harry was silent, and I looked away. We knew perfectly well why Grandma was angry tonight. I had shouted at her, acted in a way no grandchild should have acted — especially a grand*daughter*.

"Whatever Grandma is doing, we'd better find her," Harry said soberly. "It's dark, and the streets aren't safe for an old lady wandering around by herself." He looked more concerned than I had ever seen him, even on Mount Rainier.

I searched the east side of our street and Harry the west side, while Father took the car and cruised around the neighborhood. There was no group of Japanese tourists, no dinner party Grandma could join.

After an hour, we met and compared notes. Nobody had seen a trace of Grandma — none of the neighbors had, none of the passersby.

"Should we call the police?" I asked. "They can blanket the neighborhood better than we can."

Father shook his head. Although the night was cool, he had to wipe the perspiration out of his eyes. "Not yet."

"I'll call Steve," I said. "He'd be an extra pair of feet for pounding the streets."

"Good idea!" said Father. "I'll call Ellen."

With the extra people, we spread our search over a wider area. Our house was situated in the northern end of a Seattle district called Capitol Hill. It was a neighborhood of steep streets, with fine views of the lakes and the mountains. Crime was not a major problem.

The neighborhood slightly to our south was rougher, however. I didn't think Grandma could have walked as far as that. I couldn't think about it.

With Steve's help, I looked into every alley, checked into every backyard. We looked behind all the garbage cans and recycling bins.

It was nearly midnight when our search party met again and confessed failure. I was reeling with fatigue, and I saw that Ellen looked just as bad. She had been awakened out of a sound sleep.

"Let's go into the house," Father said quietly. "We'll have to decide whether or not to call the police."

In the living room, Ellen sat down on an armchair and covered her eyes with her hands. Father sat down beside her and put an arm around her shoulder. Steve and I dropped heavily onto the sofa.

"It's my fault," said Harry in a low voice. He paced back and forth. "I haven't been very nice to Grandma lately. I hurt her feelings and drove her away."

I didn't know whether to laugh or cry. Had he forgotten that *I* was the one who had ranted and raved at Grandma? He was so self-absorbed that he thought only *his* actions had the power to disturb Grandma.

"Don't blame yourself, Harry," Father said. "She went off on Mount Rainier, remember. That wasn't entirely because she was mad at you."

"Yes, she *was* mad at me," he insisted. There were actually tears in his eyes. "Instead of keeping her company, I was with this girl in the cafeteria."

"Talking like this doesn't do any good, Harry," said Father. "How about some tea?"

I suddenly felt a great thirst and started to get up, but when I heard Harry putting the kettle on in the kitchen, I sank back gratefully.

Minutes later Harry came back, holding a cup of tea in his hand and sipping. "I shouldn't have said those nasty things to Grandma about her winnings in the nursery home."

Four pairs of eyes stared at him — at the single cup of tea he had made for himself. It hadn't even occurred to him that anyone else might want some.

Ellen sputtered. "Harry, I don't believe it! Didn't it occur to you that others might want some tea, too?" She turned to Father. "What kind of family is this?"

Father looked away. "You're not seeing us at our best, Ellen. We're not usually like this."

He was wrong. We usually *were* like this, I realized. Ellen was seeing us, seeing Harry, exactly the way all of us normally were. Harry always made tea just for himself. Grandma always made the rest of us feel guilty.

Jumping up, I went to the door. "I'm going to search along Broadway. Coming, Steve?"

As we walked down the block, Steve stopped. "April, I've been thinking. I bet your Grandma is making a fool of us again. She's probably sitting in a coffee shop somewhere, chuckling to herself while she pictures her family rushing around frantically."

If only I could believe it! I shook my head and walked on. "Grandma is not playing a trick this time. She was too upset."

Steve caught up with me. "What happened?"

I had already called him earlier about being accepted at the Colorado School of Mines. We reached Broadway, the brightly lit street lined with small businesses. As we waited for the light to turn green, I told him about Grandma destroying the letter from the admissions office. Just thinking about it made my blood boil again. "It sent me into a rage. I shouted at her."

"And she was furious?"

"No — at least she didn't show it. All during dinner, she just sat there, like a block of stone."

Steve took a deep breath. "Then she's just doing this to punish you. She's paying you back for shouting at her."

I was almost convinced. "But Steve, you're the one who thought she was such a sweetheart. You said so."

"That was before I got to know her on the picnic," Steve said grimly. "Ellen was right. Your Grandma is just trying to make us feel it's all *our* fault. Besides, what she did with your acceptance letter was inexcusable. I say we call off the hunt and go home. She'll show up when it suits her, the way she did on Mount Rainier."

I remembered Grandma's quiet triumph as she finally showed up with the Japanese tourists. Of course, she was pulling off the same sort of trick. Of course, she just wanted to worry the family.

But I couldn't ignore the fact that as every minute passed, her blood sugar was reaching a more dangerous level. "I want to believe you, Steve, but I just can't take that chance."

"Look, this old woman has been manipulating you for most of your life. You know it yourself, April. This is your chance to break free!"

"It's easy enough for you to say! She might be in a coma this minute! You don't care if she lives or dies because she's not *your* grandmother!"

Steve flinched. Then he said quietly, "I can't believe you mean that, April."

Tears flooded my eyes and the streetlights blurred. Without looking at each other, we walked down the sidewalks of Broadway, crowded even at this hour of the night. It was the main drag in this part of town, and it was seven blocks from our street. That was a long walk for a woman of seventy, but she could do it if she was angry enough.

Then I thought, if Steve and I broke up, Grandma would win. Didn't she manage to break up Father and Ellen on Mount Rainier?

I tried to swallow the brambles stuck in my throat. "Steve, I'm sorry for what I said. It was unforgivable."

Steve put his arm around my shoulders. "*I'm* sorry for not remembering your grandmother's diabetes. Of course, we have to look for her."

I leaned my cheek against his chest. It felt warm, and I could hear his heart beating. If Grandma had hoped to break up the relationship between me and Steve, she had failed.

We walked on, passing punks, panhandlers, yuppies, teenagers on Rollerblades, sidewalk poets, and other characters usually found on Broadway.

"It's hard to see your grandmother joining people like these," said Steve. "Besides your yelling, did anything else happen recently to upset her?"

Panting, I tried to keep up with his long steps. "It's an accumulation of things, I guess. As Harry said, he hurt her feelings. Also, we made a visit to the nursing home to see Grandma's old friend."

Steve stopped and looked at me. "Uh-oh."

"Yes, it was an awful mistake," I said. "Grandma somehow got the idea that Dad wanted to put her in the nursing home."

"And does he?" asked Steve. "Does he threaten to send her there?"

I sighed. "I don't think there's any question of sending Grandma to the Green Haven Nursing Home, not after the way she cleaned out the residents in a mah-jongg game."

"April, you figured out what your grandma was up to on Mount Rainier. What do you really think she's doing tonight?"

Up to now, we had been rushing around frantically searching, without really trying to understand Grandma's motive. It was time to stop and think.

"After everything that's happened," I said slowly, "Grandma would feel that the whole family is against her, even Harry."

"So she'd feel rejected," said Steve. "Do you . . . do you think she might do something desperate?"

I swallowed. "Even more desperate than running out into the night?" I tried to fight down panic and think clearly. "No, what she would be more likely to do is something that would shame us."

"Is your grandmother religious?" asked Steve, as we passed a church. "Could she have gone in here?"

I shook my head. A load of tiredness suddenly fell on top of me, and I had to lean against a tree in front of the church. "We'd better go back and ask Dad to call the police, if he hasn't done it already."

Several dark shapes were crouched in the porch of the church. I shivered in the night air. It was spring. What would happen to these pathetic derelicts during the long, dark Seattle rainy season?

Could Grandma have joined this group? No, how could she? She was always so fastidious about cleanliness.

But wait! Putting herself among these people would do it: bring shame to her family. It would tell the world that we had forced her to join the homeless.

I walked up to the porch of the church and leaned down to peer at the huddled figures.

A woman's voice said hoarsely to a neighbor, "Want part of my candy bar, honey? You don't look so good."

"No, thank you," replied a faint voice. "I don't want to eat."

I jumped. The voice had spoken English with a Chinese accent!

Grandma was lying on the steps of the church, covered by a ragged quilt that she

188

shared with the gray-haired figure next to her. Gently, I pulled the quilt away and, with Steve's help, lifted her. A sour smell arose, and I nearly gagged.

"She looks pretty sick," whispered Steve. "We'd better get an ambulance."

FOURTEEN

DR. WILTON came out of Grandma's hospital room. The look on his face was reassuring. "You got to her in time. An hour later, she would have gone into shock. I've given her some insulin, but it won't be necessary to repeat the injection as long as her condition remains stable."

He smiled at me. "You're the young lady who found her, aren't you? Good thinking. You must know how your grandmother's mind works."

"Then she must be the only one!" said Father. His face was drawn. "Do you think my mother will need psychiatric counseling?"

Dr. Wilton shook his head. "She'll be all

right with some proper food and rest. Of course, you'll have to stop her tendency toward rambling, especially at night. But that's just a matter of keeping a vigilant eye."

After Dr. Wilton left, we sat down in the hospital lounge and looked at one another. Grandma's latest "rambling," as the doctor called it, was more serious than her earlier ones. The others were willful or mischievous. This one seemed desperate. She had been ready to risk coma, even death, in order to beat her family — me — back into submission.

"Grandma ran off because she was mad at me," Harry said brokenly again. He had been saying more or less the same thing for the last twenty-four hours. I felt sorry for the girl who would marry him.

"I don't know what to do," Father said dully. "April, Dr. Wilton thinks you understand Grandma better than anybody. Why do you think she's doing all these things? What does she really want?"

"I think," I said slowly, "that Grandma is a Dragon Lady who wants to be the dowager empress."

Father and Harry stared. "What on earth are you talking about?" demanded Harry.

I didn't answer. But I made up my mind to

talk with Grandma as soon as she was strong enough.

By THE THIRD DAY, Dr. Wilton decided that Grandma was well enough to go home. "She should rest in bed for a couple of days, but after that, I don't see any reason why she shouldn't be up and about. In fact, it's good for her to move around."

Caring for Grandma in her sickbed took a lot of time, but for once Harry spelled me occasionally. He still felt enough guilt about Grandma to watch over her — provided it didn't conflict with anything.

In fact, as long as she was in bed, Grandma was not much trouble. Even Ellen would probably consent to live under the same roof with her. But we couldn't keep her in bed forever.

The day came when I carefully helped Grandma go down the stairs and into the living room. She lowered herself into an easy chair.

After Grandma was comfortably seated, I pulled a footstool over and sat down facing her. This was the right moment for a talk, and Grandma seemed to be waiting for it.

I cleared my throat. "Grandma, I'm sorry I yelled at you. It was an outrageous way for a granddaughter to behave. Now tell me the truth. That wasn't the real reason why you joined the homeless on Broadway, was it? You had a plan."

"Of course," replied Grandma calmly. "I told you that we women are yin, not yang. So we can't get our way by open means. We have to do our work indirectly."

I nodded. "You managed to make all of us feel guilty. That was part of your plan, wasn't it?"

"I've earned the right to a comfortable old age," said Grandma. "And I intend to get it."

"But what does that have to do with throwing my letter away?" I demanded.

"If you went away to college, what do you think would happen to me?"

"Dad will find a way! He promised that he would do his best to take care of you."

"His best? That means sending me to the Green Haven Nursing Home!"

So she had overheard the exchange between Father and the director after all. That was why she had identified with the homeless people huddling on the porch of the church.

I remembered that Ellen, too, had hinted about the possibility of a nursing home. "Is that why are you so dead set against Dad marrying Ellen Wu?"

Grandma nodded. She paused to collect her thoughts. "My marriage to your grandfather was a typical one for my generation. It took place in Chongqing, where the Nationalists moved the capital after the Japanese had invaded our country."

What did all that have to do with Father's wanting to marry Ellen?

As if sensing my impatience, Grandma said, "You won't understand me unless you understand my background — which is also your background."

"Yes, Grandma," I said meekly. I didn't agree, but I held my tongue.

"In the forties, young people of my generation thought of ourselves as modern. But girls like me had little chance to make the acquaintance of suitable young men. Although arranged marriages were supposed to be out of date, our parents made sure that the young men we met were always sons from the 'right' families."

I still didn't see what all this had to do with Father. "Doesn't Ellen Wu come from the right family? Aren't the Wus friends of ours?"

"Be patient!" said Grandma. "You see, when a girl got married, she didn't marry just a boy — she married into his family."

This was something I had already heard from Ellen.

"When I married your grandfather, my two principal duties were to bear sons and to serve my parents-in-law. The second duty was just as important as the first."

"So Ellen Wu wouldn't make a very good Chinese daughter-in-law," I murmured.

"What do you think?" asked Grandma. "My duties included getting up at five every morning to cook the rice soup for my mother-in-law's breakfast. She had frequent back pains, and I had to give her massages in the middle of the night." She looked sardonically at me. "Do you think Ellen would do all that?"

"No, she wouldn't," I admitted. Mrs. Li might have done all that, especially if it meant that she and her son could get green cards and stay on in America.

"Only one thought sustained me during those interminable cold nights when I was massaging my mother-in-law," continued Grandma. "And it was that someday, I myself would be lying there in a warm bed, being served by *my* daughter-in-law."

She looked up at me, and her eyes were flashing. "In my old age, don't you think I deserve something better than a daughter-in-law like Ellen Wu, who buys ready-cooked food from a restaurant and sprinkles her conversation with scraps of German?"

The venom in those words shocked me. There was no way that Ellen and Grandma could share the same roof, I could see that now.

If I went away to college, what would happen to Grandma? Steve had said that it was not my problem, that Father was the one who had to deal with it. But my family was important to me. I wasn't like Harry. I couldn't selfishly pursue my own interests and go to Colorado knowing that I was leaving behind me an abandoned grandmother or a father forced to give up the woman he loved.

"HELLO, APRIL," said Ellen. She was smiling and her voice sounded cheerful, but I could see the strain in her face.

Ellen greeted Steve and then introduced the tall, bearded man by her side. "This is Jack."

We had run into them at the entrance to the University Bookstore, and we were standing in the way of people trying to get in or out.

"April, we need to talk," said Ellen. "How about coming over to my apartment? Then we won't have people tripping over us."

"I've got to run," said Jack. He smiled at me. "Nice to have met you. Ellen told me a lot about you."

He was very attractive — and that worried me. Was there a chance that Ellen and her former husband might make up?

"How is your grandmother?" asked Ellen as we walked toward her car.

"She's much better, and she's resting at home now."

Ellen's eyebrows rose. "Who's minding her? Isn't it usually your job, April?"

"Honorable Grandson Harry is doing the sitting," said Steve, grinning. "He's been quite conscientious, after Grandmother's latest escapade. It's guilt, I think."

"So I'm taking advantage of it while it lasts," I said. "I might even have the evening free, too!"

"Hey, that reminds me," said Steve. "If we're going out tonight, April, I'd better get back to Wendy's and put in some extra hours now."

Ellen's two-bedroom apartment was light and spacious. Its living-dining room combination seemed almost obsessively neat. The glass top of the coffee table had only a stack of magazines, neatly lined up.

Ellen must have noticed my surprise as I

looked around. "You were expecting cuckoo clocks from the Black Forest?" she asked.

"I've never been in a glamorous bachelor girl's apartment before," I confessed.

Ellen looked flattered. "The first time your father visited, he said he found the place intimidating. In fact, he said he found *me* intimidating."

"He has obviously changed his mind," I said, testing a very modern-looking chair and finding it surprisingly comfortable.

Ellen sat down on a matching chair. "April, what shall we do?"

"I'm glad you said 'we,' Ellen. That means you haven't written off the Chens."

Ellen's eyes were lowered. "There were times, during the last few months, when I seriously considered it. But I know I can't give Gilbert up. He means too much to me." Her voice was not completely steady.

There was still hope. "You mean a lot to him, too, Ellen."

"Maybe your grandmother can go live with your uncle Walter," Ellen said. "After all, he's her favorite son. Everybody can see that."

"I actually asked Dad once why Grandma didn't stay with Uncle Walter. He said she didn't want to. She said it was the duty of the eldest son to care for her. That's always been the way in China."

"In China, yes," said Ellen. "But this is America."

"Sometimes I don't think Grandma realizes that. Actually, I have a sneaking suspicion that she decided to live with our family because she can't get along with Uncle Walter's wife, who's pretty bossy."

"Whereas your mother was much too good-natured," muttered Ellen.

Suddenly an idea came to me. It was so dazzling that for a moment I couldn't speak.

"What's the matter, April?" asked Ellen. Her voice seemed to come from a distance.

I looked slowly around the apartment. "Ellen, do you think your place is big enough for two people?"

There was a long pause. Ellen finally broke the silence. "You mean Gilbert moving in with me?"

I nodded. "You will never be able to live together with Grandma, and Dad will never bring himself to send her away. This is the only solution."

Ellen frowned. "But how can your father leave his house and move into a little apartment like this?"

"You think it's going to be too crowded for you?"

"That's not what I mean," said Ellen. "Gilbert will be giving up that big house, which has been his home for so many years. And his belongings can't possibly all fit in here. Will he be able to do without them?"

I looked steadily at Ellen. "Why don't you ask him?"

Ellen asked. A week later, I found out what Father's answer was.

FIFTEEN

GRANDMA had gone up to bed, and Harry and I were watching the police chase some suspects on TV. Father turned the volume down. "I have some news for you," he said quietly.

I peered at Father's face and saw that he looked years younger. Maybe it was because his eyes contained a reckless happiness you saw more often in teenagers.

"Ellen and I have decided to get married," he said. Even his voice sounded younger and curiously shy.

My heart gave a great leap. So he had decided! "Good for you, Dad!"

Harry's mouth opened and closed a few times. Finally he gave a slow whistle. "You wouldn't be kidding us, would you, Dad?"

Father shook his head. "We're getting married tomorrow by the justice of the peace. I've already got the license, and two of our friends will be witnesses."

When Father wanted to, he could work fast. I felt breathless. "When are you going to tell Grandma?"

Father cleared his throat. "Not until it's all over. I think it's better this way. I know it's cowardly, but . . ."

He didn't have to spell it out for us. Grandma was resourceful, and she would be sure to find a way to derail the marriage if she had advance warning. The only solution was to present her with an accomplished fact.

"Hey, this is great!" said Harry. Now that he was getting over the shock, he began to chuckle. "Imagine, running off to get married, like some kid who is underage!"

Father blushed. "Ellen says we're eloping."

NEXT MORNING, which was Saturday, Harry and I watched Father leave the house wearing an unusually solemn expression with a tinge of guilt. It was a good thing Grandma was not at the front door to see him leave. She would have instantly suspected something.

Last night we had already talked about whether we should have a wedding party at home before Father and Ellen went off on their honeymoon in the San Juan Islands. Father had finally decided against it.

"Ellen said that she wouldn't be able to swallow a bite under the stony gaze of her new mother-in-law," Father had said ruefully.

Ellen was certainly honest, if not exactly tactful. A wedding party like that would be a gruesome way to start one's married life.

As we waited, I couldn't help wondering whether what I had done — what I had persuaded Father to do — was a betrayal of Grandma. The next minute I felt that I had saved Father and myself. Time seemed to crawl.

Then my supersensitive ears caught the sound of familiar wheels coming to a halt outside, and the opening and slamming of the car doors.

The front door opened, and Father and Ellen quietly entered the house.

Grandma looked up, and at the sight of Ellen, she froze. Father cleared his throat. "Mother, this morning Ellen and I were married by the justice of the peace."

For a moment I was afraid that Grandma might go into shock. With a great effort, she gathered herself together. "I see," she said quietly. "You're telling me that you've already done it."

That was when I saw how wise Father had been to get married first and then tell Grandma. There would be no breakdowns, no running off into the night. Those were weapons to be used to prevent this marriage from taking place. They were useless now.

Grandma slowly looked around the living room, which was filled with pieces she had brought from her own home. "I suppose you'll want to move all these things out now and replace them with Ellen's modern furniture," she said bitterly.

"No, nothing in this room will be changed," Father said gently. "You see, I won't be living here anymore. I'm moving to Ellen's apartment."

This second shock was almost as great as the first one. Grandma's face was pale. "You are running away?" she said finally.

Father sat down on the sofa facing Grandma, and Ellen sat down beside him. "You used to tell me a lot of stories about the Dowager Empress Cuxi," he began.

Grandma sat as motionless as a statue. She had told me those stories, too. The Dowager Empress Cuxi was nicknamed Old Buddha because during her tumultuous reign, no matter what disasters overwhelmed the country, she kept herself impassive like a statue of the Buddha. Grandma's face was rigidly set — just like Old Buddha's.

Father continued. "When Cuxi's son, the emperor, began pushing through reforms that she didn't like, she had him arrested and installed her grandson on the throne, a young boy who was much easier to control."

I understood what Father was saying, and I could hardly contain my glee. For years he had bowed down to his mother and tried to be the dutiful son — even though Grandma had openly favored Uncle Walter. Now he had finally stiffened his spine.

"I don't know what you are driving at," Grandma said through stiff lips.

Ellen leaned forward. "Gilbert is saying that he is abdicating. You won't have to contend with an upstart young empress like me. You are free to install your grandson, Harry."

After a pause, Grandma said, "Install Harry? What a quaint thing to say!"

I cleared my throat. "Harry is what he is

because you've made him that way, Grandma. You've deliberately made him dependent on you. You told me so yourself. Well, you're stuck with him now, and he's stuck with you."

"Hey, wait a minute!" protested Harry. "What are you getting at, April?"

"If you don't know what I mean, Harry, then you'll always live in happy ignorance, won't you?"

Harry's eyes narrowed. There was a chance — a very faint one — that one day he would catch on.

Grandma looked around at the family circle: Father, who seemed so determined suddenly; Ellen, who would never be browbeaten; me, a granddaughter who had dared to shout at her; even Harry, who might wake up one day.

Suddenly she looked old and frail. "There will be nobody to take care of me, then. What will happen to me? Are you going to put me in the Green Haven Nursing Home?"

Although she looked at Father, I knew her words were also spoken to me. It was an act! Of course, it was an act! And yet I still felt trapped. Harry wouldn't give Grandma the care she needed. With Father gone, I would have an even heavier burden of looking after her.

Then Father turned and smiled at me. "I

managed to find a Chinese widow," he said. "Her name is Mrs. Hua. She's just emigrated from China, and she doesn't speak much English. She was looking for work, so I offered her a job to come here as a housekeeper and do some cooking and light housework."

And to see that Grandma doesn't wander off into the night, I said to myself silently. I felt like someone who had just climbed out of a pit with steep, slippery sides.

Grandma was thinking furiously. I could almost see the thoughts passing through her head. This Mrs. Hua would show the proper Chinese respect for an elderly person. Best of all, Mrs. Hua might make an acceptable future daughter-in-law, in case Father and Ellen ever broke up. After all, Ellen had been divorced once, and being a demanding sort of person, she might make it a habit.

Grandma folded her hands and nodded. "Very well," she said to Father. The relief in the room was almost tangible. Someone sighed. Maybe it was me.

Father bent over Grandma and gently kissed her cheek. "Good-bye, Mother. We're going off on our honeymoon."

Ellen started to approach but stopped dead when she saw the expression on Grandma's face. Someday a bridge might be built, I thought, but not now.

After Father and Ellen had left, Harry said quickly that he had to go to the library. "I've got a lot of reading to do for my assignment, so don't expect me back in time for supper."

As he left, I heard him mutter to himself, "Goddamn! Imagine my old man having so much juice left in him!"

I washed the rice and prepared the vegetables for supper. Then I went to look for Grandma and found her standing in front of the house, blowing dandelion seeds into Mr. Saunders's yard.

She turned and looked at me. "You're telling me that you'll be deserting me, too, aren't you?"

"Yes, I'm going away," I replied. For once I felt not the slightest tinge of guilt. "I've made up my mind to go to the Colorado School of Mines this fall."

"There is a perfectly good university here in Seattle," said Grandma. "It's good enough for Harry."

"You won't miss me," I said. "You're always telling me that girls are of no value. Daughters are counted as a loss to the family. That's why you've always preferred Harry to me." The bitterness came pouring out.

Grandma slowly shook her head. "You're wrong. I love you and Harry equally."

"Then you have an unusual way of showing it."

"What do you mean?"

"You threw away my letter of acceptance, Grandma. You didn't care about my education at all. Harry's education is the only thing that matters. Harry is the only person you care about."

Grandma was silent for a moment. "You're thinking of the jade bracelet, aren't you?" she said finally. "You still remember that I told you I was giving it to Harry, for his future wife."

I nodded. Grandma looked at me, her eyes begging me to understand. "I wanted you to have it, but you'd take it away with you when you marry. The bracelet belongs to the Chen family, and society would condemn me for giving it to you."

"Chinese society, perhaps," I said. "But this is America!"

"I'm a Chinese," Grandma said softly. "It's too late for me to change."

"Chinese society is changing, too. You can change if you really want to."

"April, you're asking too much from me!"

I hardened myself. "Then, since you're expecting me to go away, it won't matter whether I go this fall or wait until I get married."

I went back into the house. I didn't look back at Grandma's face. I couldn't afford to.

OUR HIGH SCHOOL graduation ceremony took place in the afternoon, and it was held at Seattle Center. I was planning to join my friends for a party that evening, but before that, my family was having a small celebration dinner at home.

It wasn't the first time that Father and Ellen had come home for a visit, but there was still a feeling of awkwardness. Was Father supposed to sit in his old place at the end of the table, or did the position now belong to Harry? It might be a good idea to have a round table in the future, I thought.

Steve came, of course. "I've got to eat a lot to fatten up for my trip to Japan next week."

To my surprise, Harry had invited Janet, his Cantonese-speaking girlfriend. She turned out to be the reason why he went so often to study at the university library. She and Harry had been doing their math problem sets together. I should have known.

It wasn't easy to persuade Mrs. Hua, the

cook, to sit with us at the table. Mrs. Hua came to cook, as well as clean house and take Grandma for walks every day. Her manner was always deferential, and she didn't presume to call Grandma by her first name. The only trouble was, she bore an uncomfortably strong resemblance to Mrs. Li.

Mrs. Li had returned to China with her son, and we had a letter from her saying that she had remarried. Her husband, one of the new breed of businessmen in China, made money selling cassette tapes. Her son had started third grade and was at the head of his class. I was glad to hear that they were both doing well, but I still couldn't forget the poignant sight of the two of them waving good-bye to us.

Father's marriage with Ellen showed no signs of breaking up. It didn't seem likely that Mrs. Hua would become a daughter-in-law, in spite of her excellent cooking.

Father was certainly enjoying the dinner. He took three helpings of the Lion's Head dish, which Grandma had taught Mrs. Hua to make.

"You're eating like someone who hasn't had a decent meal in weeks," Grandma said to Father.

The barb was intended for Ellen, of course,

but she only laughed. "Gilbert is just learning to cook. He needs a lot more practice before he can get as good as this."

Grandma's breath hissed, but she managed to control her shock. Her face became impassive again. "We get what we deserve," she murmured.

Unexpectedly, Mrs. Hua spoke. "Many husbands in China are doing the cooking these days. Some are better cooks than their wives."

Grandma glared at her. Mrs. Hua blushed a deep red and bent over her rice bowl. She didn't speak a word for the rest of the meal — for the rest of the evening, in fact.

I wondered if she would always stay squelched. People changed, after all. Father and I had both fought for our freedom and won. Harry had dared to bring Janet home. Chinese husbands now did the cooking. Only Grandma was too old to change.

After the meal, Father took me aside. "Does Grandma still go for visits to the Green Haven Nursing Home?"

I nodded. "She goes almost every week to visit Mrs. Liang. Phyllis Liang is so grateful to us that it's positively embarrassing. Personally, I think Grandma goes for the mah-jongg. The director doesn't let them play for stakes anymore, and Grandma has even returned the hair clip. But she still likes to go."

Father nodded. "Now that she knows we aren't planning to send her to the nursing home, she probably enjoys going there for the company."

When the dining table was cleared, I opened my graduation presents. "This is beginning to feel like a shower."

From Steve I got a gadget for moistening postage stamps. It was shaped like a clown's head, and Steve demonstrated by pressing a button. A moist, red tongue stuck out. "To make sure you write," he said.

After the laughter had died down, I opened Harry's present. It was a sweatshirt with a picture of a girl holding a pickax and standing triumphantly on top of Pike's Peak in Colorado. Harry must have had it especially made to order.

Father and Ellen gave me a laptop word processor. It was the same present that Harry got when he graduated.

"That's an expensive gift for a girl," remarked Grandma. But she said it automatically, as if her heart wasn't really in it.

Ellen, however, bristled. "Don't worry, Mother," she said acidly. "I helped to pay for it."

Finally I came to Grandma's present. It was a small, flat package, wrapped in thin tissue paper. I felt the shape of the object inside when I picked it up. Hardly daring to breathe, I tore open the tissue paper. Inside I found the jade bracelet.

I was wrong: Grandma was not too old to change after all. I raised my eyes and saw that she was smiling at me.